| DATE DUE | | | |
|---|---|---|---|
| | | | |
| | | | |
| | | | |
| | | | |
| | | | |
| | | | |
| | | | |
| | | | |
| | | | |
| | | | |
| | | | |
| | | | |

**11762**

F
WAL

Wallace, Karen.

The unrivalled
Spangles

# THE UNRIVALLED SPANGLES

## KAREN WALLACE

ATHENEUM BOOKS FOR YOUNG READERS

New York London Toronto Sydney

*To Diane, with love*

Atheneum Books for Young Readers

An imprint of Simon & Schuster Children's Publishing Division

1230 Avenue of the Americas

New York, New York 10020

Cover design by www.blacksheep-uk.com copyright © 2005 by Simon & Schuster

Originally published in Great Britain in 2005 by Simon & Schuster UK Ltd.

Published by arrangement with Simon & Schuster UK Ltd.

Book design by Christopher Grassi

The text for this book is set in Vendetta Medium.

Manufactured in the United States of America

First U.S. edition 2006

2 4 6 8 10 9 7 5 3 1

Library of Congress Cataloging-in-Publication Data

Wallace, Karen.

The unrivalled Spangles / Karen Wallace.

p. cm.

Summary: Longing to give up the nineteenth-century English circus life she was born into, sixteen-year-old Ellen Spangle secretly prepares to be a governess and is courted by a wealthy young man until two tragedies lead her to reevaluate her plans.

ISBN-13: 978-1-4169-1503-4

ISBN-10: 1-4169-1503-6

[1. Circus—Fiction. 2. Self-perception—Fiction. 3. Family—Fiction. 4. London (England)—History—19th century—Fiction.] I. Title.

PZ7.W1568Unr 2006

[Fic]—dc22 2005026478

# ONE

ELLEN SPANGLE SAT ON HER HORSE'S BACK AND WAITED FOR the musicians to finish their introduction. It was always the same. The music played on until the audience were just about frantic. On the horse beside her, Lucy suddenly scrambled to her feet. "Let's go in standing!" she cried.

"No!" cried Ellen firmly. "We'll do what we rehearsed!" She looked at her sister's flushed face. Even though they had waited in the wings a hundred times before, the music always had the same effect on Lucy as it did on the audience. By the time they went into the ring, she was on the verge of losing control. "You'll put out the band and Father will be furious."

"Who cares about Father?" Now Lucy was standing up. She was fourteen and thought she knew everything.

"I do," said Ellen, who was sixteen and more cautious than her sister. "And so do you, when you bother to think about it." She grabbed Lucy's arm and yanked her down. "You go first!"

Lucy fixed her sister with her bright green eyes.

"Are you sure? I went first last time."

"Of course," said Ellen. The first great roar of the crowd

didn't matter to her. But it mattered desperately to Lucy. For Ellen the challenge of performing was doing it well. For Lucy it was the thrill of being adored.

A trumpet played a single note. A second trumpet joined, followed by a third. Together the notes sounded like the rhythmic pounding of horses' hooves. It was the cue for their act.

Lucy slipped back into the saddle and blew her sister a kiss. Then she threw back her head and galloped into the ring.

Ellen took a deep breath. The air was hot and smelt of horse dung, orange peel, and sweat. From the wings she saw the huge gas chandelier blazing with hundreds of glowing jets. She heard men, women, and children shouting at the tops of their voices. She felt the wooden floor of the theatre shudder with the banging of heavy black boots.

Ellen urged her horse forward. It was always the same. There was a jolt of nerves and excitement as she plunged into the crowded, brightly lit theatre.

Fred Spangle strode across the sawdust. He was a short, powerfully built man in a scarlet ringmaster's tailcoat with a glossy black top hat. He snapped his whip in the air. "Ladies and gemmen!" he cried in his rich, booming voice. "All the way from the palaces of Italy—the pride of kings and the wonder of princes—I give you *The Amazing Scarletta Sisters*!"

Ellen watched as Lucy capered around the ring. Her frothy sequined skirt fell over Chestnut's glossy haunches like a golden waterfall. She gathered her reins in one hand and held her arm up in the air. The band changed their tune.

Ellen fell in behind her sister. Twice they cantered around the ring, then Ellen moved up beside Lucy and they swung themselves onto their knees and up onto the backs of their horses. The gold of their skirts picked up the gold braid on their tight satin jackets. In one smooth movement they took each other's right and left hands. Below them the horses had fallen into exactly the same stride.

Together, they jumped over poles streaming with ribbons. It was as if they were joined at the hip. Then Ellen slipped back into a seated position. A second later Lucy did the same. Now they followed each other through fiery hoops with one stride between each jump. When they had circled the ring twice, they pulled up their horses and bowed.

A huge smile was fixed on Ellen's face. She waved her arms in the air. She turned and bowed. The crowd roared as the two sisters curtseyed together. Ellen smiled wider, but inside she was screaming. Lucy *was* Seraphina Scarletta. Ellen would never be Sapphire Scarletta.

Early the next morning, Fred Spangle walked across the frosty mud of Fender's Field near Whitechapel in the East End of London. It was only just dawn. Behind him a row of show wagons huddled in the shelter of the broken brick wall that separated the field from a muddy lane and a row of grimy, tumbledown cottages. On the other side of the field there was a cluster of wooden shacks and a circle of the heavy carts and drays that held the animal cages above the damp of the winter mud.

Fred stopped and smelt the sharp whiff of ammonia that wafted from the cages and mixed with the peat smoke from the first of the morning's fires. In the cold weather, he always wore a long, thick sealskin coat and high, black leather boots. He looked more like a general inspecting his troops than a showman patrolling his circus.

Around him, wagon doors creaked open and men and women stumbled into the pale dawn light. They stretched stiff limbs and rubbed their hands over crumpled faces. Women hung kettles over smoking fires as if they were walking in their sleep.

Everyone saw Fred but no one called out greetings. Most of them had been with Spangle's Circus for as long as they cared to remember. It was a hard life, but the only one they would ever choose to live. Fred Spangle was a fair employer but a tough one. There was work to get on with, and Fred's temper in the morning was well known.

Somewhere in the murk on the far side of the field, a hyena screamed and a lion growled. It was feeding time. A man's voice cursed as a tin pail rattled against the bars of a cage. Fred carried on walking but grunted approvingly. Animals came first in his circus.

Across from the field, on the other side of the muddy lane, a girl stood wrapped in a grey blanket. "Buns! 'Ot and tasty! Three for a penny!"

Judy Currant, they called her. Her pitch was on the top steps of the crumbling theatre where Spangle's Circus performed in the winter. Fred quickened his step and felt for a penny in his pocket. For some reason he hadn't slept well after last night's performance. Now he was particularly hungry.

Five minutes later he climbed up the steep steps to his own showman's wagon and pushed open the brightly painted door. A single paraffin lamp swung from a hook on the low ceiling. The floor was covered with a worn woven rug, and two large frying pans hung above a small cast-iron stove. In the far corner of the wagon, he saw his elder daughter bent over some sewing. Unlike her sister, Ellen was an early riser. Fred's coat made him so wide he had to turn sideways to get through the narrow doorway.

"Blimey," he muttered, half to himself. "That lion of ours got a bigger cage than we have."

A woman looked up and smiled. She was handsome rather than pretty, and her glossy black hair was pulled into a loose roll. Norah Spangle tipped a saucepan of steaming cider into a tin mug and took the buns he held out to her.

"Maybe he does, but I doubt you'd prefer his breakfast." She sipped her own mug of tea. "Has his cough improved?"

Fred sat down on a bench along the wall. He dunked his bun in the hot cider. "Ludwig says so."

As he spoke, he pulled a face, half from the cider that burned his tongue and half from the memory of his animal keeper just before dawn that morning. He had been standing outside Claudius's cage playing a violin. He stank of the brandy kept for the animals' colic attacks.

The lion seemed soothed by the music—indeed he looked as if he was listening to it. But Fred knew as well as any circus man that a drunken keeper was a danger to himself and the animals in his charge. If Ludwig Klemper hadn't been the best animal trainer in England, Fred would have sent him packing ages ago. It was only a matter of time before Claudius chewed off his arm instead of listening to his violin.

Norah looked up at the outline of her husband's face against the only window in the wagon. He had barely changed in the eighteen years she'd been married to him. His hair was still the colour of amber, and his eyes were the greenest she had ever seen on a man.

Fred held out his mug and gave his wife a sideways look. "Will Lorinda the Lion Lady go on tonight?"

Ellen Spangle looked up from the net skirt she was darning. "Is your ankle strong enough, Ma?"

It was not a question her father would think to ask. It wasn't his way. If you fell off your horse, Fred made you get back in the saddle. If you took a bad tumble, Fred made you do it again until you got it right. If you turned your ankle like her mother had done, you hobbled through your act.

That was circus life.

Norah Spangle knew that her husband was worried about takings. Although last night the theatre had been full, circuses usually made almost all of their money when they toured the countryside in the summer. In the winter, they had to live on what acts they could cobble together. Ellen and Lucy as Sapphire and Seraphina Scarletta were a big draw. But a lady lion tamer was always a crowd pleaser, and Norah Spangle was the best in the business.

"Your liniment has worked wonders, dear." Norah patted her daughter's hand.

"Adder fat's best for sprains," said Ellen. She smiled. "I'll never know why."

"If *you* don't know, no one else will." The hot cider had softened Fred's face. "You're a clever lass. It was a good act last night."

Ellen looked down. It wasn't often that her father called her clever or complimented her on her riding. If he did, it was usually said with a sneer. If Fred had had his way, neither she nor her younger sister and brother would have been taught to read or write. In his view, you didn't need learning in the sawdust ring.

Ellen had heard his bad-tempered views on education a hundred times. *Only leads to bad words chalked up on every gatepost. Got so a decent woman can't venture out of doors.*

Luckily for Ellen, her mother had other views.

"Who pays the suppliers?" Norah would shout. "Who writes the orders? Not you! My life would be a damned sight easier if I could keep proper accounts and say what I mean on paper." Then there would be the bang of a saucepan on the table and a clatter of cutlery. "My children are not going to have to pay a clerk if they want a decent letter written!"

In the end, even though Fred sulked and shouted by turns, Norah arranged for a tutor to teach her children first thing in the morning, before they practised their acts and groomed their horses.

The problem was that the only child who had really *wanted* to learn was Ellen. Lucy, who was barely eighteen months younger, had resented every moment. But then Lucy was her father's daughter. She had Fred's amber hair and green eyes and the same views on education. What was the point? Better to spend the time perfecting her riding skills or learning how to juggle with the Indian clubs that Fred had bought for her last birthday. They had come all the way from Bombay. Lucy loved breathing in the spicy smell of the painted wood. So, as soon as she was thirteen, Lucy had talked her mother into letting her give up the lessons. Now only their youngest brother Sam, who was just ten, still took them. But Sam always had other things on his mind. His pig Curly was almost ready to show. His two teams of white mice had learned how to pull their coaches in a circle in opposite directions. Ellen was teaching him to train small animals to live together in a "Happy Families" cage without eating one another. People in the street couldn't get enough of them. For a penny, they would stand and gawp at a cat, a rat, a ferret, and three canaries all in one cage, watching one another as if their lives depended on it. Which, of course, they did.

Sometimes Ellen wondered if she had the same blood in her veins as her brother and sister. For Lucy and Sam, it was enough to be called Spangle and to spend the rest of their lives with the circus. It wasn't enough for Ellen. Her father could sense her dissatisfaction but couldn't make head nor tail of it, which infuriated him. Ellen was a natural performer. More than his other children, she had inherited her mother's extraordinary talent with animals. Fred reckoned it was because Ellen had shared a straw-filled box with a pair of orphaned lion cubs when she was a baby. It had been a bitterly cold winter, and the cubs' box had been the warmest place to be.

"Sam says you've tamed that ferret of his." Fred Spangle patted his stomach. "No more rabbit pies for me now, I suppose."

Ellen stared stupidly at her father. She was so lost in her own thoughts she couldn't think what he was talking about.

"Sam's Happy Families Cage," said Norah quickly. It wasn't often that her husband and her eldest daughter had a conversation that lasted more than two minutes. She wanted to do anything she could to encourage it.

Ellen smiled ruefully. "It took five rabbits, two canaries, a sharp pin, and a noose."

"Sounds about right to me."

"I'd say that ferret will behave himself now," she said.

She and her father were both smiling.

From her place by the stove, Norah felt a pleasure she hadn't known for months. It was a terrible thing in a circus family when a father and daughter battled each other all the time. But it seemed to Norah that for some reason things were better—and she didn't know why.

Ellen decided to take advantage of her father's good humour. After a week of grey days, this morning was turning out brighter. She would be able to sell as many pots of liniment as she could carry in her basket. More importantly, she could pay her tutor Alfred Montmorency what she owed him for her last lesson.

When Ellen was fourteen and her lessons finished, Fred had immediately tried to blot out all the things she had learned. He made her practise twice as long, so there was no time left in her day to read. If he saw a book in her hand, he threw it into the fire.

But Ellen had inherited his stubbornness. Nothing was going to stop her from learning. In the summer she toured with the circus and collected plants and powders for her potions and liniments. When the circus came back to Fender's Field for the winter, she sold her medicines and used the money to pay for lessons from Alfred Montmorency. For the past two years, she had secretly learned Latin, Greek, and English literature, and she had been given an introduction to the natural sciences. Now this winter would be her last. After the spring she would be old enough to apply for a job as a teacher or a governess.

Neither Fred nor Norah had any idea of this arrangement, but Ellen couldn't hide it from Lucy. The two sisters shared a room in lodgings near the theatre, so there could be no secrets between them.

"It would be a shame for a hardworking showman to go

hungry," said Ellen as she wrapped her paisley shawl around her shoulders. "And it's a fine day for selling." She picked up her bonnet and slid her arm under the handle of her basket. "I shall buy you a steak-and-oyster pie from Minnie's."

Norah looked up. "Would you buy me a card of pearl buttons and three yards of red satin for Lucy's costume?"

Ellen's face fell. Now she wouldn't be able to pay Alfred Montmorency.

Norah looked at her daughter's disappointed face. "I'll make it up from the takings, dear," she said in a puzzled voice.

Ellen told herself to be more careful. Her mother missed nothing. "Anything else, Ma?" she asked quickly.

Norah shook her head and picked up the skirt that Ellen had been mending.

A moment later Ellen was walking through the narrow alleyway past the Spangles' theatre and into the crowded cobbled street. Even though it was still early in the morning, costermongers and flower ladies were hurrying to their pitches.

"Where are you going in your new shawl?"

It was Lucy. Her cheeks were pink from the cold air and her crinkled auburn hair fluttered about her face.

"You're up early!" said Ellen.

"I bought some red satin for my costume," said Lucy. "I promised Mother weeks ago I would, but I've been too busy practising." She twirled daintily on the balls of her feet. "Where are *you* going?"

Ellen nodded at her basket. "What do you think?"

"You'll be selling your liniment, then settling with Alfred Montmorency."

"That's clever of you," said Ellen lightly. Now that Lucy had bought her own satin, Ellen could pay off her debt. "Perhaps you should take up mind reading."

The two sisters stared at each other. Lucy didn't approve of Ellen's lessons. She couldn't understand how Ellen could possibly want a life outside the circus.

"You're cracked!" Lucy would shout. "Who's going to employ a circus girl to teach their children? You'll be sweeping the grate and blacking the steps, more like."

Last summer the circus had visited Cambridge during a hiring fair. Lucy had heard all the stories from the country girls looking for jobs.

"Mop fairs, they call 'em, Ellen," she sneered. "'Cos that's what you have in yer hand, all day and half the night. Not a book! Governess! Pah!" Lucy would grab Ellen's arm and stare at her with her mad green eyes. "Stay with me! We'll be famous! We'll go anywhere you want!"

Then Ellen would pull back and try to explain to her sister yet again that she wanted her life to be different. Being part of a circus separated you from the real world. Only a fellow performer understood that there was nothing glamorous about riding bareback around a brightly lit ring in front of hundreds of people. It was hard work and harder than most. But the real reason why circus folk tended to stick together was because they knew how to live with their different identities. People on the outside would never understand that Ellen Spangle was not Sapphire Scarletta, and that made Ellen feel like a freak. Worse, she knew that no one was even interested in Ellen Spangle. They only wanted Sapphire Scarletta. But Lucy never listened. "You've got the circus in your blood, Ellen," she whispered. "You're just too stubborn to admit it."

Now Lucy grabbed Ellen's hand and began to speak quickly. "Come with me! I want to show you what I've been practising. No one's done it yet. I could teach you, too."

Ellen's heart sank. "Lucy," she said gently, "you're already a sensation. Everyone adores you." Ellen set down her basket. She knew exactly what Lucy was practising. It was true that no one had done it before, but for good reason. A forward somersault on a galloping horse was almost impossible, and extremely dangerous. Everyone had warned Lucy not to try it.

Everyone, that is, except Fred Spangle.

"Lucy," began Ellen. She put her hand on her sister's arm. "I beg of you—"

"Don't beg," snapped Lucy. "It doesn't suit you."

Before Ellen could reply, Lucy ran off, holding her hands out on either side as if they were wings. Ellen picked up her basket. It felt heavier than before.

"Zat one," said a voice beside her. "If she was my horse, she would get no more oats."

It was Ludwig Klemper, the animal keeper. *"Comment allez-vous, Mademoiselle?"*

Ellen smiled at Ludwig's dark, lined face. He had an enormous moustache that was waxed into perfect twirls at either end. *"Très bien, merci, Monsieur. Et vous?"*

"Bah!" spluttered Ludwig suddenly. *"Ça marche. C'est tout."* His breath reeked of brandy.

Ellen rolled her eyes. "You've been drinking again, Ludwig."

The wiry animal trainer stared hard at Ellen. He was trying to make the two Ellens he could see merge into one. "It's ze elephants," he cried. "Colic. A whole bottle." He sighed. "It is hard to keep elephants happy."

"We don't have elephants anymore."

Ludwig bowed in front of the two lovely young women standing before him. *"Vous êtes très gentille, Mademoiselle Ellen. Les éléphants vous remercient."*

Ellen watched Ludwig stumble away, using the crumbling brick wall of the theatre as a guide. She shook her head. There was no understanding Ludwig sometimes, though he was the cleverest man she knew. She remembered the time she had watched him train a kangaroo.

It was when her lessons were finished and her father had taken her books away. Afterwards Fred had gone to an animal fair to buy two broad-backed horses. In the circus they were known as resin-backs because of the powdered resin that was sprinkled on their haunches. It was one of the tricks riders like Ellen and Lucy used to keep their grip when they stood up in their leather-soled slippers. When the horse deal was done, the horse trader's cunning eye had noticed a sovereign left over in Fred's hand.

"Want a hopping boxer? He's sick, so you could have him cheap."

Fred Spangle had never owned a performing kangaroo. But he knew they were a good draw. "How sick?"

"I ain't a doctor." The horse trader jerked his head sideways. "'E's in the sack there."

Two hours later Fred and Ludwig heaved the sick kangaroo out of its sack onto the summer grass.

"Whatchya think?" asked Fred.

Ludwig looked down at the animal's miserable hunched body. Its heavy-fringed eyes were dull and blank. Ludwig ran his hand down the kangaroo's back. The fur was thin and sticky and the ribs stuck out like fish bones. The kangaroo didn't even twitch, let alone try to defend itself.

"Too early to tell."

"Do what you can. I'm a sovereign down."

Three weeks later the kangaroo was called Lord Rowley and was hopping about tethered on the end of a long rope, grazing happily in the field. He was glossy, fit, and lazy.

It was then that Fred Spangle began to get impatient. "When's that kangaroo going to box for me?" he asked Ludwig every other day.

And every other day, Ludwig said the same thing. "He'll box when he's ready."

"Either that animal boxes or he's lion food," hollered Fred one morning.

Ludwig had turned to Lord Rowley and looked into his bright brown eyes. "That animal means what he says," he said.

Lord Rowley looked back. *Why should I bother?*

"Bother or you're in bits," said Ludwig.

Ellen had been standing in the empty tent when Ludwig led Lord Rowley into the ring. They both wore boxing gloves. She watched in amazement as Ludwig sidled up to the kangaroo and punched him on the nose.

The kangaroo was outraged. He jerked upright and began making stabbing movements with his forelegs, which looked as if he was boxing because of the leather mitts tied to the ends. Ludwig hopped around him, aiming punches but making sure not to hit him. The more punches Ludwig aimed, the more Lord Rowley tried to punch back.

"So you can box after all, my Lord Rowley!" cried Ludwig. "Congratulations! The lion will be disappointed!" As he spoke he pulled out a large handful of fresh grass from his pocket and waved it in front of the kangaroo's nose.

After a moment's hesitation, Lord Rowley ate it.

Ellen stepped out of the shadows. "How did you know he would eat the grass?"

"Because he thinks he's won!" Ludwig bowed to the kangaroo and fed it more grass. "He thinks I'm paying him a tribute." For a split second Ludwig looked into Ellen's face. "What he *thinks* is the important thing."

֍   ֍   ֍

Now, as Ellen stood on the cobbled street and watched a coalman's cart rumble noisily past her, she thought of what she had learned that day. Ludwig always said there was nothing much to choose between people and animals. They all had their funny habits. The trick was to find out what they were and turn them to use.

The next day Ellen had engaged the services of Alfred Montmorency.

As for Fred Spangle, he thought he saw a new acceptance in his daughter's manner and was sure he had done the right thing by burning her books.

# TWO

ALFRED MONTMORENCY SAT IN THE CORNER OF AN INN CALLED the Sheaf of Barley and sipped a mug of thin beer. He looked at his watch. He was waiting for his friend, Edward de Lacy, and as usual, Edward was late. Around him, the room was crowded and stank of wet wool. Men with red faces muttered and nodded at each other over heavy wooden tables. Someone burst out laughing and stamped his boots on the floor. Alfred gulped at his beer. He was so used to his own company that loud noises or outbursts of any kind made him nervous. It embarrassed him when people made a show of themselves.

Alfred looked up and found himself staring at his own reflection in a huge mirror with a broken wooden frame. The face that stared back was heart-shaped with a dimpled chin and inquiring eyes behind round, steel-framed glasses. His brown hair was thick, parted to one side, and brushed in a shiny swoop over his forehead. The shine came from the only extravagance Alfred allowed himself—a daily application of Heale's Sandalwood Scented Pomade, made exclusively by Morris Heale & Sons, of Jermyn Street.

It was what his father had used all his life. It was what Alfred had used every morning since his father had died ten years before.

Alfred ran his fingers over his hair and held them discreetly in front of his nose. He breathed in the rich, musty smell of the pomade. Everything about his father had been lavish and exotic. All his clothes and shoes and hats were handmade by the finest outfitters in London. When he travelled, he went first class. When he stayed in hotels, he took the best suite.

As a child, looked after by a governess and a nanny, Alfred had cherished the postcards his father always remembered to send him. He imagined him travelling on luxury paddle-boat steamers. He pretended he could taste the mint tea his father might be drinking in the palm-shaded gardens of white hotels with pink marble floors. One day he would do the same.

But Conrad Montmorency invested all his money in a silver mine, which turned out not to exist. He lost everything. When he heard the news, he promptly died of a stroke.

At the time, Alfred and his mother had assumed that while there would not be the funds to maintain the same lifestyle, they could expect a modest income. If they had to do without a second parlour maid, at least they would be able to keep a roof over their heads. But they were wrong. Conrad Montmorency's extravagant lifestyle had left his family entirely bankrupt. Mrs. Montmorency was forced to sell the house she had lived in all her married life. She had to watch the ornaments and paintings and furniture she had come to love fall beneath the auctioneer's gavel, without the means to buy back a single memento.

Alfred sighed and pushed the memories from his mind. Oddly, he felt no bitterness towards his father. When the disaster happened, Alfred had been able to continue his education at the finest schools and universities through scholarships and bursaries. Now that he had come down from Oxford, he had been able to keep himself with his tutoring and even send a little bit of money to his mother in the cottage she rented in Sussex.

And of course there was his novel. The novel would be a triumph when he wrote it. Alfred had no worries about his ability to write. And he knew that one day he would be a success. All he needed was a good story. Alfred was patient and observant. One day it would come. He sipped at his beer and thought instead of the morning's events. They had started with the discovery that he had finished the last of his pot of sandalwood pomade. For the first time since his father's death, he couldn't afford to buy another one. The daily use of the pomade was a ritual that connected Alfred to his father. The idea that the ritual would now be broken distressed him enormously. Then the young woman who called herself Pearl Rowley had arrived with the money she owed him.

Alfred had been surprised to see her. Miss Rowley had warned him that she might not be able to pay him until their next lesson. At the time he had assured her that this would not inconvenience him. But as soon as the money was in his pocket, he had put on his overcoat and started out on the journey to Piccadilly. On his return he had found a note from Edward de Lacy suggesting they meet for lunch.

Now the frosted-glass double doors of the tavern swung open and Edward strolled into the noisy room. Alfred, with his shabby woollen jacket with its patched leather elbows, had the authentic look of an impecunious scholar. Edward, however, affected the dress of a struggling painter with a singular lack of success. His baggy tartan trousers, while crusted with mud from the streets, were too glossy. His cream silk shirt and floppy red necktie had the unmistakable crispness of garments recently plucked from a mahogany hanging cupboard. And his green corduroy jacket had the velvety sheen of a clothes brush briskly applied by a trained valet. Unlike Alfred, Edward's hair was fine and blond and flopped into his face. And his blue eyes usually showed no interest in the world around him.

Today, though, Edward's eyes were gleaming. If he had been on his own he would have hugged himself, he was feeling so excited. He liked meeting Alfred for lunch. They swapped accounts of recent adventures and discussed the meaning of life. Edward never tired of such discussions, and he loved telling stories. But now something else was on his mind.

Edward had just turned the corner of Lion Street, where Alfred lived, when a young woman walked out of his door.

Edward could see immediately that she was in some kind of disguise. Her bonnet was faded and she wore an old-fashioned paisley shawl. Even her black boots were the heavy, button-up kind.

Edward was thrilled. Alfred had always told him his pupils were schoolboys struggling with examinations or, in exceptional circumstances, middle-class young ladies who wished to impress their friends on their afternoon visits—apparently, these days, a well-judged quotation could make a pleasing impression in discerning households. But the young woman who stepped out of the door fell into neither of these categories. She was simply the most beautiful creature Edward had ever seen. But it was more than her beauty that had struck him. There was something exotic about her. She couldn't hide it under the faded bonnet and old-fashioned shawl.

Edward *felt* this. But even though it was only a feeling, it buried itself deep in his mind and began to take hold of his imagination. He decided not to knock on Alfred's door. He didn't want to appear flushed and agitated when Alfred came out, so he scribbled a note and handed it to the servant girl.

As Edward moved through the crowded room, Alfred noticed him immediately. He bumped into tables and almost knocked over mugs. Alfred watched as men followed his progress with a look of faint irritation. The man was as large and clumsy as a wolfhound puppy. Alfred's heart sank. Edward was in one of his exuberant moods.

"Edward!" Alfred stood up and shook his friend's hand. "I was delighted to get your note. How are you?"

"Intrigued, Alfie. Fearfully intrigued." Edward threw himself down in the opposite chair and knocked the table so Alfred's beer mug wobbled.

"Something for you?" A greasy barmaid appeared beside them with a dirty napkin over her arm. "Hot rum and water?"

"Capital," cried Edward. "Two large glasses!"

"I'm happy with beer," said Alfred.

Edward shook his head. "Certainly not. My treat. And two of your best pies!"

The barmaid wiped the table with her dirty napkin. "Steak-and-oyster do you?"

"Perfectly."

Alfred frowned. He had taught himself to do without a midday meal a long time ago. Besides, the pomade had cost him more than he expected.

Edward was grinning. "I'm bribing you, you chump!"

"I beg your pardon?"

Alfred wished now that he had not agreed to the meeting. He had known Edward since his school days. Although they were completely different, they had stayed in touch even when Alfred's circumstances had changed so dramatically and Edward's father had become more and more successful as a society physician. Alfred knew that Edward was expected to follow in his father's footsteps and go to medical school. But his mother, Lady Amelia de Lacy, had other plans. For the moment she was bored and Edward, her only son, was her favourite toy.

It was Lady Amelia who had encouraged Edward to follow the artistic life. She paid for his painting lessons. She chose most of his clothes. Artists were so much more interesting than doctors, and since it was Lady Amelia's family and money that had been her husband's introduction to society, she felt he owed her this time. The fact that Edward showed no talent as a painter didn't bother her in the slightest. His artistic pretensions allowed her to invite the most fascinating people to her visiting afternoons. Anyway, she couldn't imagine him away at a university cutting up dead frogs to please his father.

Edward gulped at the glass of hot rum that had been set down in front of him. "Tell me more about your mysterious pupil."

"What mysterious pupil?"

"The beautiful girl I saw outside your house this morning." Edward wiped his mouth with a handkerchief. "In disguise. A lady, obviously."

He peered into Alfred's uncomfortable face.

"Ha!" crowed Edward. "Just as I thought! A mystery!" He nudged Alfred's untouched glass towards him and nearly tipped it into his lap. "Drink up, dear chap. Tell all."

Pearl Rowley had been Alfred's pupil for two years. She had come to him through the recommendation of a second-hand bookseller they both knew. After they had discussed her requirements, she had looked him straight in the eye. "I would be obliged if you kept our arrangement confidential, Mr. Montmorency. I have nothing to hide, but my circumstances are unusual."

It had never occurred to Alfred to do anything other than honour her request.

Now he shrugged and looked into Edward's pale, sweaty face. "There's nothing to say. She shows a remarkable talent for reciting Keats's poetry and for healing terriers." As he spoke, he could hear her voice: *I cannot see what flowers are at my feet, Nor what soft incense hangs about the boughs.*

Alfred had never heard such a lovely voice.

"Healing terriers?" Edward spluttered and his rum sprayed across the table.

Alfred tried to control his dismay. How dare Edward pump him for private information? But Alfred knew from experience that the only way to make Edward tire of a new game was to pretend to play along with him. If he refused to speak, Edward would only become insistent and then sulky.

Alfred shrugged. "She wrote to me and arranged for a lesson at noon one day a week." He swallowed a gulp of rum and water and felt the hot alcohol go instantly to his head. "Jasper was ill with a bad back. He was in such pain I had almost decided to drown him. She put her hands on his back, and a moment later he had recovered."

It had been extraordinary. Pearl Rowley had laid the terrier over her lap and worked her fingers down the length of his spine. When she put him back on the floor, his legs were working again, and Jasper was wagging his tail.

Alfred gulped again at his glass.

"What's her name?" Edward almost whispered.

"Pearl Rowley." The moment he said her name, Alfred was furious with himself. The rum had loosened his tongue. He had broken a promise. He must do everything to discourage Edward's curiosity.

"Has she been a pupil for long?"

"Barely a month. I doubt she'll be back."

"You said she comes for lessons at noon," persisted Edward.

"I did not," replied Alfred too quickly. "Besides, her sort never keep up their arrangements."

"What do you mean, 'her sort'?"

Alfred picked a word that least applied to Pearl Rowley. He had never seen such a determination to study. "Dilettantes. Books are baubles to them."

But Edward wasn't listening. With a child's cunning, he was sure Alfred was lying. He had already made a plan. He would make a point of coming to Lion Street at noon for the next two weeks and wait for the lovely girl to come back. He knew from previous conversations with Alfred that most of his pupils had weekly lessons. Then he would follow her and discover the true reason for her disguise. Edward's heart thudded in his chest. What an adventure! How *thrilling*!

Alfred watched Edward's face, and the steak-and-oyster pie sank in his stomach like a lump of stone.

ⓢ　ⓢ　ⓢ

"Roll up, roll up, ladies and gemmen! See the Famous Chinese Swinish Philosopher! He casts spells. He performs tricks. He tells fortunes! Roll up! Roll up!"

It was a week later and Sam Spangle stood, nervous and excited, on a wooden box at the entrance to Fender's Field. He wore a black tunic with silver braid and a conical hat. A long pigtail woven out of horsehair was pinned to the back of it. At his feet his pig, Curly, also wore a conical hat strapped to his head and sat on the edge of a circle of wood chippings. Curly had been trained to walk and stop at the faintest tap of a cane. Today was his debut.

"Roll up! Roll up!" shouted Sam. "Straight from the palaces of China! First ever performance!"

A good-sized crowd had gathered in front of him. It was a fine day, and many people had come to look at the posters for the circus's evening performance.

"Get on wiv it, lad!" cried a lady with a purple face under a purple bonnet.

Sam jumped down from his box. This wasn't quite how he had imagined Curly's first performance, but there were enough people now, especially if they all put a penny in his cap when the show was over.

Sam passed his hands in front of his face. He pulled five silk handkerchiefs out of thin air. "Watch carefully, ladies and gemmen! You are about to see a miracle!" He tied the scarves around Curly's eyes. "Who's got a penny?"

"Go on, Harry!" screamed a scabby-nosed girl.

A youth with a sour face threw a penny into the wood chippings. Sam watched where it landed and surreptitiously tapped his cane against the side of his boot.

To the crowd's amazement, the blindfolded Curly set off around the ring.

"Cor!" cried the lady in the purple bonnet. "'Oo'd have believed it?"

Round and round went Curly, but no penny was found.

"Gimme back my penny!" squawked the young man called Harry.

A cackle of laughter spread through the crowd. Right at the back Ellen watched her brother proudly. What a little showman he had become. He knew exactly what he was doing.

"'E's lost my penny," bawled Harry in an agonised voice.

Sam pulled a mysterious Chinaman's face. He tapped his cane twice against his boot. Nobody noticed. They were all watching Curly. Mysteriously, Curly stopped.

"My Swinish Philosopher never fails!" Sam strode over to where Curly had stopped. "Ladies and gemmen, pray silence!"

Sam knelt on the ground and picked up a penny that he slipped down his sleeve.

"Thank you, sir," he cried, bowing to the astounded Harry. "And another for your favour!"

The crowd clapped good-naturedly as Sam put two pennies into the man's grimy hand.

Fred Spangle had had no idea Sam was planning to show

Curly's tricks that day. He knew the boy had been training the pig, but not that they had worked up an act. As he was crossing the field, he had seen a small crowd and stopped to find out what was going on. Now he watched his son with swelling pride. The boy was brilliant. Where had he learned all those fancy words? Then he saw Ellen's face on the other side of the crowd. Of course, she'd taught him. Her and her books. Fred looked again at the enjoyment on the faces in the crowd. The right patter was half the battle. Maybe he could turn Ellen's fancy words to good business. Fred chuckled to himself. Then his chuckle died away.

Two gypsy women had walked up to the edge of the ring. They were dressed in flowing silk skirts and embroidered waistcoats. Their eyes glittered like their gold jewellery. Circus people and gypsies never mixed. Wild animals, was Fred's view. Cunning, dangerous, and vicious.

Sam saw the gypsies too, and his heart sank. Sure enough, the people around him were getting edgy. A gypsy could have the clothes off your back and you wouldn't notice. Sam thought fast. If he lost his punters before he could pass round the cap, he would make nothing and lose a penny into the bargain.

"Ladies and gemmen!" cried Sam. "A Swinish Philosopher shall tell a gypsy's fortune!" He stared at the younger of the two women. "Step forward, dear lady, and consult the oracle of the Orient."

At that moment Lucy passed by. She saw the gypsies and

understood the problem. What Sam needed was a diversion. She pushed through the circle of people and stood between Curly and Sam. "I'll know my fortune," she cried.

"From a pig or a gypsy?" asked a scratchy singsong voice.

The older woman stepped up to Lucy and grabbed her hand. Lucy tried to pull it away, but the gypsy's grip was too strong. She had flattened Lucy's palm and was already peering at it.

Fred Spangle roared up to the front of the crowd. "I'll have no slippetty-sloppetty gypsies here," he bellowed. "Be off, the pair of you!"

Ellen found herself staring at the gypsy woman's face. The eyes were hooded and flecked with yellow. Suddenly the woman's face flinched, and her eyes widened. She dropped Lucy's hand as if it were a hot coal. And in a swirl of bright silk, both gypsies were gone.

A cold horror spread through Ellen's body. What on Earth had the gyspy seen? Fred would be furious that Lucy had allowed her hand to be taken. But it had happened so fast. What else could she have done? Ellen turned quickly away before her father had a chance to yell at her.

"There you have it, ladies and gemmen," cried Sam desperately. "What good's a gypsy's chatter against the skills of a Swinish Philosopher?"

But it was too late. The crowd had melted away. When Sam looked around, Ellen was gone.

On the other side of the field, Fred was shaking his fist at Lucy.

၆ ၆ ၆

Ellen ran from Fender's Field. She walked wildly through the cobbled streets. Gypsies were liars and fakes. She knew that. But the look on the woman's face as she held Lucy's hand loomed in her mind like a monster in a nightmare.

She looked up. Around her, the houses and shops had changed. They weren't brick and wood anymore, but stone. An omnibus clopped past. Ellen stopped. She had no idea where she was. The street was almost empty. It was noon. She passed a tavern called the Sheaf of Barley. Outside a man was selling hot pies from a tall metal stove. She walked to the end of the street to find a street sign and get her bearings.

The sign said Lion Street.

To her dismay, Ellen realised she was standing a few yards from Alfred Montmorency's door. She held on to the railings to get her breath back. Then she hurried away, hoping that Mr. Montmorency would not choose that moment to take his dog for a walk.

Alfred Montmorency didn't see Ellen. To Jasper's despair, he was crouched over a table writing his novel.

At the other end of the street, Edward de Lacy's heart leapt in his chest. What excellent fortune! He allowed himself a smirk of triumph. That would teach Alfred to try and throw him off the scent! It had been a close-run thing, nevertheless. Yesterday Alfred had appeared before Edward had a chance to hide. All he could do was bend down and pretend to tie up his shoe. At the time, he was sure that Alfred had recognised him. He had hesitated. Then, to Edward's profound relief, he had kept on walking.

Now the hunt was on!

Edward followed Ellen's dark green woollen skirt as it disappeared back down Lion Street and around the corner. He kept as close as he dared. He didn't know the East End, so every turning she made was a mystery to him. At first he thought she might be making her way to the omnibus stop in Whitechapel Gardens. It was the fastest way to make the journey back to town. But it soon became clear that she wasn't going that way, so all Edward could do was follow her. After twenty minutes, his legs were aching with the effort of keeping up, and he noticed to his consternation that each street became more run-down and dirtier than the one before. Perhaps the poor girl was lost herself?

"'Ere, mister. Please, mister. Wot you following that lady for?" A ragged boy with a face like a starving chimpanzee scuttled beside Edward and tugged at his jacket. "I'll catch her up if you want." The beady eyes glinted knowingly. "Save you the trouble, like."

"No, no," gasped Edward. "Don't do that. I beg of you."

"A sixpence says I won't," said the boy, quickening his pace. He took another look at Edward's face. "Nah, make that a shillin'."

"That's blackmail!" spluttered Edward. He couldn't believe it. The child couldn't be more than seven years old.

"Your choice, sir," snapped the boy. "Ask the lady, shall I?"

Edward held out a shilling and pulled back as the boy's filthy paw touched his hand.

"Nice doin' business wiv you, sir!"

Edward had only taken his eye off the street for a second, but the mysterious girl was gone.

His stomach felt as if it was full of ice cubes. He ran down the filthy street as fast as he could.

It was a dead end. In front of him was an open field with half a dozen circus wagons and two or three rickety wooden buildings. A group of horses and two donkeys stood huddled in a group. Beside them, a kangaroo with a woollen blanket over its back was tethered to the ground. Edward looked up the street. There was an ironmonger's shop, three brick lodging houses, and an old theatre hung with painted billboards. He looked the other way. A row of dirty hovels slumped against each other like a line of broken bricks. There was a coal dump at the end of the street.

He walked up towards the old theatre. Two men in clown makeup strode past. "'Oo's swallowing the flames tonight, you or me?" said one. The other tossed three Indian clubs in the air and caught them. "You!"

The first clown skipped to one side, slapped the soles of his feet together. "Then you feed that stinking hyena."

Edward ducked behind the pillar and found himself looking up at the painted billboard. A pyramid of acrobats towered over three silver-suited tumblers. Two girls balanced like ballerinas on the backs of two horses. SAPPHIRE AND SERAPHINA, THE AMAZING SCARLETTA SISTERS. Edward's eyes travelled over the face of the first girl. She had red hair and green eyes. The other sister ...

He clutched the pillar. The other sister was the girl he had seen outside Alfred Montmorency's house!

Edward's whole body trembled with excitement. His mysterious beauty was a circus rider! He stared at Ellen's long, beautiful face. But what kind of young woman would ride in a circus and study Greek and Latin? And—what had Alfred said—recite Keats's poetry? Edward hopped up and down and hugged himself.

On the omnibus home to Notting Hill, Edward relived again and again the moment he had looked at the painted billboard. His whole body fizzed with excitement.

A secret! His very own secret!

It was too wonderful for words!

## THREE

"WHAT'S THE POINT OF 'EM?" ASKED SAM SPANGLE, LOOKING AT the bouquet of roses. "Even Lord Rowley wouldn't eat 'em." He bent down and pushed his nose into the red petals. "They don't even smell."

It was three weeks later, and Ellen was sitting with her family in the small room behind the stage where the props were stored. The last performance had just finished and they were all still wearing their costumes.

"What's the point of them?" said Sam again, nudging the roses with his foot.

Fred chuckled and patted his son's thick black hair. "You'll understand when you're older." He winked at Lucy. "It means your sister's got an admirer. A gentleman admirer, no less." He walked over to a small chest of drawers and took out a flat, green leather box. "He left this for you too. I put it in the drawer for safekeeping."

Fred held the box out to Lucy, but she didn't take it. "They're not for me, Pa. It's Ellen as has the admirer."

Fred stared at his younger daughter. For three weeks the flowers had been arriving after every performance of The

Amazing Scarletta Sisters. It had never occurred to him that they might be for anyone other than Lucy.

"But those gloves you were wearing last week—"

"Ellen gave them to me," said Lucy. She loosened her scarlet satin jacket and stepped out of her sequined net skirt.

"Why would I need a pair of red kid-leather gloves?" said Ellen lightly.

The atmosphere in the room became more edgy by the minute. Norah felt her temper rising. At first the flowers had been flattering. Admirers were part of circus life. She had had many in her own time. But when gifts of silk handkerchiefs and soap and gloves arrived, she began to feel uneasy.

"Lucy doesn't need them either," said Norah harshly. "Better swap a pair of kid-leather gloves for a pair of boots and some woollen stockings."

"Or a new cage for my mice!" cried Sam, who suddenly saw how he might turn his mother's disapproval to his advantage. "I've trained ten now!" His eyes bored into the green leather box in his father's hand. Even the box looked expensive. "Isn't anyone going to look inside?"

"That's up to Ellen," said Norah Spangle firmly.

Ellen took the green leather box from her father. She was as uneasy as her mother, although neither of them had spoken of it. Like her father, she'd been certain the roses were meant for Lucy. Then Lucy had ripped away the tissue paper and found a tiny white envelope with "Sapphire" written on it.

Inside the envelope had been a thick white card edged

with gold. "From an Admirer" was written in bright red ink.

"Red and gold for our costumes!" Lucy had forced herself to laugh. "What a subtle admirer you have!" She stopped. "I bet it's that tutor of yours."

Ellen shook her head. "He doesn't write like that." She ran her finger along the flowery copperplate letters. It looked more like a woman's hand.

"What shall you do with them?"

"Give them to the flower lady," Ellen had said. "She might get sixpence." Then she'd picked up the bouquet and jammed it into a bucket of water. Just as she'd done every night since.

Now Sam watched as his sisters and his parents avoided each other's eyes. He couldn't understand what all the fuss was about. Someone was sending Ellen flowers. What was wrong with that? And if he sent her presents as well, so much the better. Sam sighed impatiently. He desperately wanted to know what was inside the flat green box.

"Maybe it's a dead spider." Sam lowered his voice. "Or maybe it's three live ones!"

Norah reached out to cuff him, but he was too quick for her. "Blimey, Ellen," he said, suddenly fed up. "Open it up, for gawd's sake."

Ellen flipped the catch on the box and found herself looking at her own face in a tiny silver hand mirror.

"Lemme see!" cried Sam.

Sam took the mirror in his hands and pulled faces in the

glass. "I could buy ten cages for the price of this." He looked imploringly at his sister. "Can I pawn it?"

"Do what you like," said Ellen. She wrapped her shawl around her shoulders and untied her satin riding slippers. "I don't want it."

"Well, I do!" snapped Lucy. She grabbed the mirror from Sam's hands. As he snatched it back, it slipped through his fingers and smashed on the wooden floor.

For a moment no one spoke. Then Lucy screamed at Sam. "Now look what you've done! Bad luck, that means!"

"I didn't do nothing," Sam shouted back. "It was you." He turned to Norah. "You saw her, Ma, didn't you?"

Norah stared at the broken mirror with a frozen face. "Shut up, the both of you!"

Sam turned to Ellen. "Can I have the frame?" he whispered.

"Take it," said Ellen. "Perhaps something good will come of it."

Sam bent down and put the frame in his pocket. He had been expecting his father to object, but Fred Spangle said nothing.

Lucy spoke in a halting voice. "I'm sorry. It's my fault. I—"

"It was an accident," snapped Norah. "It's done with."

But they all knew about luck in the circus. You couldn't do without it. No one believed Norah. And she didn't believe herself.

§    §    §

Later, Lucy turned over in the bed she shared with Ellen. "I'm sorry about your mirror. I was jealous. It was stupid of me."

Ellen curled up in a miserable ball and said nothing.

"Ellen," whispered Lucy again. "Don't take it so hard. *Please*." Her voice was brittle.

Ellen knew that at any minute her sister would have a sobbing fit. "It was an accident," she said. "Let's forget all about it."

"Yes, let's!" whispered Lucy. There was silence, then Lucy spoke again. This time her voice was edgy and excited. "Ellen! I have to tell you something. But you mustn't tell anyone else. It was partly why I wanted your mirror."

Lucy's eyes were huge in the milky light of the moon, shining in through their tiny window. She hugged herself and rocked from side to side.

"Is something wrong?" Ellen asked.

"No, no. Not wrong. But first you have to promise."

All Ellen wanted to do was sleep. The broken mirror had upset her deeply, and she could see that her father was devastated. Fred was superstitious, even by circus standards. The flash of a magpie's wings would have him huddled in his wagon for hours. Ellen sat up in bed.

"I promise."

Lucy grabbed Ellen's hands. "I have a sweetheart!"

"But you're only fourteen," Ellen cried.

"Ma was fourteen when she met Pa," said Lucy in a sulky voice.

"But they weren't sweethearts," cried Ellen. "They hardly knew each other." She felt her cheeks go hot as she spoke. It didn't seem proper to talk about her parents like this. Now Lucy went rigid and sullen. She dropped Ellen's hand and pushed her away.

"Who is he?" asked Ellen in a dull voice. She didn't want to know, but she knew Lucy was going to tell her anyway. The sooner she found out, the sooner she could get some sleep.

"Joe Morgan," whispered Lucy.

Ellen's stomach turned over. "Not Jeremiah Morgan's son?"

Lucy nodded furiously. "That's why I made you promise. Pa would be mad as a bull if he ever found out."

*Madder*, thought Ellen. Jeremiah Morgan and Fred Spangle hated each other with a fury that would never be resolved. Jeremiah was the owner of Morgan's Menagerie, and there wasn't a dirty trick he wouldn't play to steal an audience from Fred. In the beginning Fred Spangle had ignored him. Morgan's Menagerie wasn't in the same league as Spangle's Travelling Circus, but over the past two years things had changed. Jeremiah had taken on more and more circus acts, and he didn't care if his posters advertised acts that didn't exist. All he wanted was the crowd and their money.

It had all come to a head last summer, when Jeremiah had sent two of his men into Chester to rip down Fred's posters advertising Spangle's Circus for the next day and put up his own. That night the two columns of men and wagons had met head-on along the country road leading to the town, and a fight had broken out between them. In the noise and confusion, two of Fred's elephants had panicked and broken free from their harnesses. The animal cage they had been pulling tipped on its side and a precious hyena had broken its back and died.

The fighting was only brought under control by the local police, and as a result both Jeremiah and Fred had had to pay a hefty fine for disturbing the peace. Fred had sworn then that if he ever set eyes on Jeremiah Morgan again, he would give him the thrashing of his life.

Ellen felt sick as she watched the silly, secret smile on Lucy's face. Marriages between circus families always caused trouble and sometimes feuds that led to parents and children never speaking again. Jeremiah would know only too well that if Lucy married Joe, Morgan's Menagerie would gain a first-class horse riding act, while Spangle's Circus would lose one of its main attractions. And if Jeremiah had found out about Lucy's friendship with Joe, he would be sure to egg them on. Ellen wouldn't be surprised if he hadn't already tried to bribe his son to rush Lucy into a decision. A shiver passed through her. Her own mother had been abandoned when she left her family's circus to marry Fred. And such was the anger and sense of betrayal that even on his deathbed, Norah's father had never forgiven her.

"Where did you meet him?" asked Ellen in a choked voice.

"Last summer in Ludlow," said Lucy. She grabbed Ellen's hand again. "Remember? We set up one night, and Morgan's followed us?"

Ellen remembered. It was well before the incident at Chester, but it was the first time Jeremiah Morgan had sent his agent ahead to pull down all the Spangle's posters and put Morgan's ones in their place. At that time Fred hadn't realised that Jeremiah was so dishonest. But when Spangle's arrived, Morgan's had already been given the best pitch, and even though Fred's was the better circus, their takings had been halved. The next day had been a Sunday, and Fred had announced that they wouldn't leave until the Monday morning instead of the usual end-of-day packing up. It wasn't to give his people a rest, though. He wanted to shake off Jeremiah Morgan.

"I wanted to see the zebras that were on Morgan's poster." Lucy laughed at the memory. She obviously had no idea that even her presence at the rival circus would have been seen as a betrayal by their father. "So there I was, gawping at them in their cages, when this clown comes up to me and tells me that zebras have wings that come off. But they are very delicate, so they are kept in a big box." Lucy snorted with laughter. "And I believed him!"

Sometimes Ellen wondered if she would ever understand her sister. Lucy had lived with animals all her life. How could she be taken in by such a trick?

"So he said, do you want to see them? And I said yes. And do you know? It turned out the zebras weren't zebras at all. They were donkeys painted with black and white stripes." Lucy put her hand to her mouth and giggled. "Anyway, I followed him round the back of the tent and—"

"He didn't—?" cried Ellen, feeling more and more horrified.

"Certainly not," snapped Lucy. "Joe would never do that." She danced her fingers along the top of the blanket. "Mind you, what's wrong with a kiss?" She paused. "But we did make a promise—"

"What kind of promise?"

"To see each other when we came to London." There was a sly look on Lucy's face. "Morgan's isn't that far, you know. They're pitched in Porlock Green."

Suddenly Ellen realised what Lucy wanted. While Ellen was allowed out on the streets on her own, Norah was much stricter with Lucy. Occasionally Lucy got away with it if she went out first thing in the morning, but on the whole Norah kept an eye on her all the time. Sure enough, Lucy's voice softened into a wheedle. "You have to come with me, Ellen. Mother won't let me out on my own."

"Lucy," cried Ellen. "Don't you understand that if anyone saw you with Joe Morgan, they'd tell Father and we'd both get a beating? And then he'd *never* trust us again."

But Lucy wasn't listening. She linked her fingers together, and from the look on her face, Ellen knew she was pretending to hold hands with Joe Morgan. Ellen had no choice but to fall in with her sister's plan. Lucy had kept Alfred Montmorency a secret. Now she was calling in the favour.

"When do you want to go?" muttered Ellen.

"Not for a bit," replied Lucy happily. "When the weather

warms up." She huddled into the pillow. "I want him to miss me."

A few minutes later she was asleep.

Ellen lay at the very far edge of the bed. Every muscle in her body felt stiff and sore. There was no point in closing her eyes. She knew now she would never sleep.

Two weeks later Fred Spangle went away to a horse fair in Kent. It was Norah's idea. Their resin-backs, Chestnut and Pearl, were getting old, and Lucy and Ellen's act was becoming more and more demanding. Ludwig had warned Fred that the horses wouldn't last after the next summer tour. It was time to think about training up their replacements if they were going to keep up the Scarletta Sisters as their star attraction. Norah played her trump card: "We don't want Jeremiah Morgan on our patch again." But it was more than getting the better of Morgan's Menagerie—Norah wanted Fred away from Fender's Field. Ever since Lucy had dropped the mirror, a terrible gloom had descended on him, which he hid behind a temper that grew shorter and more vicious each day.

Sam tried everything to cheer up his father. One morning he wheeled over a tank full of goldfish and showed Fred how he had tied the fish to a fleet of tiny wooden ships with the finest silk thread.

"Look, Pa!" cried Sam. He was very pleased with himself and his face shone. "It's the world's first miniature naval battle!" He tapped the side of the tank. As the fish darted nervously through the water, the tiny ships appeared to be sailing in a complicated formation.

"Ladies and gemmen!" cried Sam, grinning at his father. "May I present the fantastical historical goldfish! In front of your very eyes, the Battle of Trafalgar as it happened on that fateful day."

Ellen was watching, and she burst out laughing. Sam was right. It looked exactly as if the ships were sailing into a battle.

"Stop wasting your time on daft tricks!" snarled Fred. He kicked over the tank. "Get on with your tumbling or you'll be no good to me this summer!" He stomped off while Ellen and Sam went down on their knees to pick up the shiny orange bodies flapping helplessly in the mud.

"I hate him!" said Sam in a choked voice. He looked down so Ellen couldn't see his face.

"It'll pass," said Ellen quietly. "Try to stay out of his way."

One day Norah couldn't bear Fred's temper any longer. "You'd serve us better choosing horses than bullying everyone in sight," she snapped at him. "Go to the fair. We can cope without you."

So it happened that the day Edward de Lacy decided to present himself, Fred Spangle wasn't there.

For three weeks Edward had sat in his studio trying to paint a picture of the young woman he knew as Pearl Rowley. Every night she performed, he made the trip down to Whitechapel. He sat in the same seat and stared at her. Afterwards, just before the performance ended, he held up his cloak around his face and left her red roses with a circus hand at the stage door.

But no matter how hard Edward tried to draw the shape of her body or the muscled curve of her horse's neck, the lines on his canvas looked stiff and clumsy. In truth, Edward couldn't have painted a convincing lamppost. But he preferred to be a bad painter than any kind of doctor. So he kept on trying. Occasionally, when he became hopelessly frustrated with his dreams of Pearl Rowley, he tried to write to her. But he couldn't express what he felt, so he sent her presents instead. It was the only way he could think of to make her understand that her admirer was someone special.

Sometimes Edward thought of telling Alfred what was happening to him. Indeed, he wondered whether it would help him understand the confusion he was feeling. But something warned him away from telling Alfred. He was almost positive that Alfred would disapprove of his behaviour. Edward had a sinking feeling that Alfred had recognised him the time he pretended to be tying up his shoelace in the street and for reasons of his own had elected not to stop. Now the thought of Alfred's quiet, serious face irritated Edward. He would keep Pearl Rowley his secret. If he told Alfred, everything would be ruined.

Even so, as the days went by Edward became more and more agitated. Sending presents wasn't enough. He got tired of just watching Pearl perform and trying to paint her.

He longed to meet her face-to-face—and not just as a circus performer. He wanted to confront her as the young woman who took lessons in Greek and Latin grammar and who recited Keats's poetry. He wanted to see the startled look in her eyes. Most of all, he wanted to hear the sound of her voice.

Voices were very important to Edward. All his life his mother and his nanny had read him stories, and the sound of their voices had soothed him and led him into the land of delicious make-believe. It was the only place he really felt safe. He had been assured many times that the sound of his own voice was smooth and pleasant. And all the time, lately, he imagined the sweet, low notes he would hear when Pearl Rowley spoke. He had to find out for himself.

One Saturday at the beginning of February, Edward heard a blackbird sing for the first time that year. All night he had dreamt of Pearl Rowley. He couldn't bear it any longer. He dressed carefully but casually in checked wool trousers and a dark jacket with a soft, flat-topped hat. He told the parlour maid he had an appointment with a gallery owner. Two hours later he was picking his way carefully over the rutted, muddy ground of Fender's Field.

Jake Naples was juggling five silver balls when he saw the young gentleman standing awkwardly in the middle of the field. He caught the balls one by one and went over to him.

"You lost your way, sir?" Jake was a stocky little man with a grimy face and red-rimmed eyes.

Edward stared at the silver balls that lay in a row in the crook of Jake's arm. He was entranced. "How did you learn to juggle like that?"

Jake grinned and showed two metal front teeth. "Practice, sir." He cocked his head. "You wantin' someone?" He watched Edward's startled face. "Or just lookin' about?"

Edward took a deep breath. "I've come to see Mr. Frederick Spangle, if you please."

Jake tossed the five silver balls up in the air again. "Not at 'ome."

Edward looked away to hide his shock. This wasn't how he had imagined things at all. In his version, Fred Spangle had grasped his hand in a hard, rough-skinned grip and clapped him on the shoulder in a manly fashion. Indeed, Edward had been trying out a firm handshake of his own on a rolled-up bath towel at home. After shaking hands, the two men had looked into each other's faces and approved of what they saw. Then Fred Spangle had agreed to introduce him to Pearl Rowley.

Edward tried not to stare hopelessly at the stocky juggler. "I've come to pay my respects to Miss Pearl Rowley."

"Ain't no Pearl Rowley here either," replied Jake. He gave Edward a curious look. "There's an 'oss called Pearl and there's a kangaroo called Rowley. Well, Lord Rowley to the punters."

Now Edward was completely confused. "But you must know her!" he cried plaintively. "She . . . she's also called Sapphire Scarletta."

"Sapphire Scarletta!" Jake threw back his head and laughed. "That ain't Pearl Rowley, whoever she is. That's Ellen Spangle, the boss's daughter."

Edward gaped at him and tried to make himself think clearly. If the young woman had given her name as Pearl Rowley to Alfred, then it was vital she never knew Edward had mentioned it. Otherwise she would tell Alfred, and he was bound to warn her he had been spied on. Then she would almost certainly refuse to see either of them again. "Of course, Miss Spangle," stammered Edward. "I was thinking—"

"I'm sure Mrs. Spangle will be 'appy to talk to ya," interrupted Jake.

"Mrs. Spangle?" croaked Edward. "Will Miss Spangle be there too?"

"Miss Spangle ain't here either," said Jake grinning broadly. "She went off this morning to do some shopping."

As soon as Norah saw the well-dressed gentleman stepping awkwardly through the mud towards her wagon, she knew he was the one who had been leaving flowers for Ellen. Norah sighed inwardly. She recognized Edward's kind. They clustered round a circus like moths around a flame. She had known many as a young woman; but in those days, such gentlemen would never dream of forcing an introduction.

Norah was relieved that Fred was away. He would have blamed this young man for the broken mirror and doubtless sent him off with a curse for his trouble. However, experience told Norah that if she refused to receive him, such a persistent young person would only look for other ways to win Ellen's attention.

*He'll tire of her*, she said to herself. *They always do.* Reluctantly Norah made up her mind that if Ellen wanted to meet this young man, she would not stand in her way. Anyway, it was too late for objections: Ellen was walking across the field towards her.

"Pray God he tires of her quickly," muttered Norah to herself.

Ellen ran her fingers through the blue and mauve silk ribbon she had bought from Mrs. Swire's haberdashery shop to trim her old bonnet. She'd decided to start work as soon as she was back. It would keep her busy while her father was away. Then she noticed a well-dressed young man talking to her mother. Ellen stopped dead in her tracks. In Fender's Field, he stuck out like a top hat on a dung heap. Nervously, Ellen tried to tell herself that it was a clerk from the Borough Council or an engineer asking about sewers or an out-of-work actor looking for a job as a clown. But she knew perfectly well he was none of these things. Ellen's stomach turned over. This was the man who was sending the roses.

At first she was cross. It was one thing for this young man to come to see her perform. Anyone could do that. All they had to do was pay their money. But it was another to seek her out in her own home. Hadn't he caused enough trouble already? Ellen felt the colour deepen in her cheeks. Well, she was glad he had come. Now she would get rid of him once and for all.

Edward had his back to the field, but when he saw the look on Norah Spangle's face change, he turned around.

Ellen found herself staring into a man's face that was beautiful. She had never seen a face like it before. It was refined and delicate, yet had the innocent look of a child. His eyes were blue and set wide. His lips were full under a fine-boned nose. A hank of blond hair fell over his face.

"Miss Spangle," stuttered Edward. His chest was so tight he could hardly breathe. "My name is Edward de Lacy. Please forgive this dreadful intrusion. I—I have the greatest admiration for your talent, and after much thought, I felt it my duty to tell you in person."

To her astonishment, Ellen was enthralled the moment he opened his mouth. It was the elegance of his speech as much as the roundness of his voice. Against all her better judgment, Ellen felt a curiousity grow inside her.

"I am delighted to meet you, Mr. de Lacy," she replied. She smiled. "And honoured to be so admired."

Edward thought he was going to swoon as he looked at Ellen. The girl's eyes were so dark, and they sparkled like jet. Her voice was deep, yet smooth and musical. It was exactly the voice he had imagined. Edward's blood roared in his ears. He was entranced.

Edward turned to Norah Spangle. "May I have the honour to take tea with Miss Spangle? Next Saturday, perhaps?"

"I would be willin', Mr. de Lacy," said Norah slowly. "That is, if Ellen agrees."

"Tea would be most refreshing," said Ellen. She couldn't believe the words that were coming out of her mouth.

Edward took a deep breath. "Shall we meet here?"

"I daresay Mrs. Hallward's Tea Room might be more suitable," said Norah. She glanced quickly at Ellen. *You don't want the whole world knowing your business.*

Ellen came to her senses. Of course her mother was right. She turned to Edward. "Mrs. Hallward's is a very respectable establishment, Mr. de Lacy."

Edward bowed. "I should be delighted to meet you there." He went bright red, bowed again, and walked quickly away.

For a moment mother and daughter watched as the well-dressed young man picked his way around the worst of the ruts in Fender's Field. A couple of circus hands stared at him, but only for a moment. They'd seen all sorts wandering about before now.

Edward crossed over the street and turned up an alleyway.

"Thank you, Mother," said Ellen when he was gone. "I'm sure it's foolish of me, but I must admit I am rather intrigued by him."

"Clearly."

Norah was beginning to regret her decision. She knew the young gentleman would be taken with her daughter, but she hadn't expected Ellen to be so obviously fascinated by him. She suddenly wished that Fred had been there. She walked up the steps into her wagon. Then she sat down at the table. Ellen followed her.

"Mother, if you don't approve..."

"It's not a question of approval, Ellen. There are some things you must find out for yourself." Norah looked into her daughter's face and saw herself almost twenty years before. "You of all people would never believe me otherwise." She pulled out a folder of bills and uncapped the inkwell. "Now go and find Lucy."

"Lucy?" said Ellen. "What has Lucy got to do with this?"

Norah sighed. "It would not be proper for you to meet Mr. de Lacy on your own."

Ellen felt the blood rising to her face. "Are you suggesting Lucy should be my chaperone?"

"I am insisting on it," replied Norah. "Firstly because you are a respectable young woman, and secondly because I am hoping that Lucy will learn not to make the same mistake herself."

Ellen stepped back as if she had been slapped.

"So I'm a circus girl with ideas above her station?" she cried. "Is that what you mean?"

"Don't be ridiculous," snapped Norah. "You must have a chaperone and Lucy—"

"Lucy!" interrupted Ellen angrily. "She's the only one you care about."

"That's not true, Ellen," said Norah wearily. "Lucy is the only one I *worry* about. There's a difference. Now leave me alone before I change my mind!"

ꕙ ꕙ ꕙ

"I knew it! I knew it!" shrieked Lucy. She capered around the cramped, dark room in the lodging house. "A black cat crossed me in the street *and* I found a sixpence." She squeezed Ellen's hand. "You and your fancy man have brought me good luck!"

"He's *not* my fancy man!" Ellen glared at her sister. "What do you mean, good luck?"

"Now I can meet Joe." Lucy danced from foot to foot. "It's the best luck ever. You get your freedom and I get mine!"

Ellen frowned. "You mean you won't be my chaperone?"

"I'll go out of the gate with you. I'll go down the street." Lucy clicked her fingers. "As soon as we're round the corner, we're on our own."

"Lucy!" Ellen felt her temper rising. "Didn't you listen to a word I said about Father and Jeremiah Morgan? What if someone saw you?" She turned away from Lucy's bright, infuriating face. "Besides, I can't lie to Ma!"

"Who's going to lie?" asked Lucy sharply. "She'll never know. As for Jeremiah Morgan, that's Father's concern, not mine! And anyway, you're the one who's always going on about wanting your freedom. Now you can get a taste of it."

"But Edward's a gentleman!" cried Ellen. "I can't possibly meet him on my own. What would he think?" She sank into their one saggy chair and buried her head in her hands. "I'm sorry, Lucy. I can't do it. I would rather not meet him at all."

"What about me and Joe?" snapped Lucy. She mimicked

her sister's voice. "You see, I do rather want to meet Joe."

Lucy stared at Ellen's white, crumpled face. "I tell you what. I'll sit with you for twenty minutes, make an excuse, and leave. Surely that's respectable enough?"

Ellen shrugged. Lucy always said the first thing that came into her mind, and then she did whatever suited her, no matter what promises she'd made. Nothing had changed since they were children with one bar of chocolate to share.

*I'll give you the biggest bit if you give me first bite.*

Lucy had always managed to swallow the lot "by mistake."

"Goodness' sake!" cried Lucy crossly. "Mrs. Hallward's Tea Room is stuffed with nice young ladies sitting on their own with nice young gentlemen. What's wrong with you?"

"Oh, shut up!" said Ellen. But she knew they had made an agreement.

# FOUR

As soon as they had woken that Saturday morning, Lucy had insisted that she take charge of Ellen's appearance for her meeting with Edward de Lacy.

"Don't be silly," said Ellen. "I have one good dress, which is perfectly suitable."

Lucy opened the cupboard. "And I have one that is perfectly lovely."

She held up a fitted midnight blue jacket and matching waistcoat. Underneath, a softly bustled skirt was made of finer striped wool. It was simple and elegant and exactly what Ellen would have chosen for herself.

"Like it?" asked Lucy.

Ellen opened her mouth, but Lucy covered it with her hand.

"Don't ask! It's to pay you back for all the presents you gave me."

"But—"

"I said no questions! Oh! I forgot!" She reached into the cupboard again and took out a pale grey silk blouse with a delicately pleated front and a high collar. Ellen couldn't believe her eyes. Where on Earth had Lucy found such clothes? But she didn't ask. Lucy loved dressing up, and she knew all sorts of shops where the owners were happy to save special outfits for the beautiful girl with the sparkling green eyes. Besides, to ask would ruin the moment, and since Lucy had been difficult and pettish all week, Ellen was happy to leave things as they were. She laced up her bodice and pulled on her petticoat. Then she put on Lucy's new outfit.

The clothes could have been made for her.

"Now your hair," commanded Lucy. "Sit."

"Am I not to be allowed a mirror?"

"No."

Lucy twisted Ellen's black hair into in an oval-shaped bun at the back of her neck. She left a few loose curls to frame her face.

"Bonnets are out of fashion," she said as she reached under the bed and pulled out a hatbox. Inside was a small velvet hat trimmed with blue feathers. She pinned it firmly on top of Ellen's head and fetched the mirror.

Ellen stared at her reflection. She barely recognised herself. The small hat and the high collar of the blouse gave her long face a fineness and grace she didn't know she possessed.

Lucy kissed her sister on the cheek. "Now you look as beautiful outside as you are inside!"

While Ellen practised a ladylike walk in her new clothes, Lucy quickly dressed and fixed her own hair. She parted it in the middle and piled it in thick curls on the top of her head.

Then she stepped into a dark green dress with a lacy shawl collar and tied a black velvet ribbon around her neck.

Lucy turned sideways so Ellen couldn't see her. She peered into the mirror and pursed her lips into the shape of a kiss. She looked irresistible and she knew it.

There was a hard *tap* on the door and Sam Spangle walked into the room. On Saturdays he always brought Ellen and Lucy hot bread and dripping for their breakfast. The three of them ate together, and he always ate most of theirs. Now he took one look inside the tiny room and knew he would be eating the whole lot.

Sam threw himself on their bed and stared at his sisters. "Ellen looks like that picture of Ma after she'd married Pa, and Lucy's the spitting image of Gran Spangle."

Ellen smiled at her brother. "We're off in a minute, Sam. So breakfast's all yours."

Sam looked curious.

"Don't ask," said Lucy quickly. "And you won't be disappointed."

Sam shrugged. "Who's disappointed? I'll take some to Jake." He picked up his greasy parcel and ran out of the room.

"Stop frowning," said Lucy as she and Ellen walked down the street half an hour later. "It gives you lines on your face." Lucy patted her sister's hand. "I bet you're feeling nervous! I would be if I was you!"

Ellen *was* feeling nervous. In fact, despite her fine clothes, she was beginning to think better of the whole arrangement. While Lucy had been happy with the agreement they had made, Ellen had fretted about it all week. It was dishonest and she knew it.

A dustcart trundled past them. Its driver was hunched over the reins, staring gloomily at his horse's thin haunches. Around them beggars picked through piles of rubbish left over from the night before. As Ellen turned away, a filthy tramp raised his hat and smirked at her.

"I can't do it, Lucy," said Ellen suddenly. "Let's go home!"

"Go home!" cried Lucy, astounded. "Don't be daft!" She waved her arms around the squalid street. A drunken woman lay on a doorstep. At her feet, three dirty children fought over a box of rotten cabbages. She knew exactly what had upset Ellen. She felt a fraud in her fine clothes, surrounded by filth. "This is Rotten Egg Lane, for heaven's sake, you know what it's like."

She tightened her grip on Ellen's arm. "Mrs. Hallward's Tea Room is in Castle Square. It has subscription libraries and paper merchants and boys selling buns. *Nice* people go there! Please, Ellen, don't give up on me now! I know what you're thinking and you don't look like a tuppenny-ha'penny flower girl. You look almost *nobby*."

She said it so seriously that Ellen suddenly snorted with laughter.

"What's so funny about that?"

"I'm not laughing at you," said Ellen. Now she felt edgier than ever. "It's just—"

"Don't tell me!" Lucy threw away Ellen's arm. "I'll never understand you. Never in my life."

They turned a corner into a small square. Everything changed, just as Lucy had said. Here there were flower sellers and skinny boys carrying trays of muffins. A hansom cab rattled past with two pretty young women inside.

Lucy pointed to a small shop on the corner. MRS. HALLWARD'S TEA ROOM. BEST QUALITY FOR DISCERNING CUSTOMERS was painted in shiny gold letters on a brick background. It had square-paned windows and white lacy curtains tied back with bows. "Now are you happy?"

Ellen watched the hansom cab stop. The two young women stepped out and went into the tea shop.

Lucy jerked her head sideways. Edward de Lacy was walking up the street reading a book. "Here he comes," she said quickly. "Go inside and find a table. You don't want him to see you on the street."

Ellen stared at her sister. "You promised you'd come with me!"

"I want to see Joe," snapped Lucy. She walked away quickly, knowing that Ellen would not call out and risk drawing Edward's attention.

Ellen bit back tears of fury as she opened the door to the tea room. There was an empty table in a bay window. She sat down and watched Edward de Lacy buy a buttonhole from a flower seller. He fitted it into his jacket. Ellen's heart started to hammer in her chest. Any minute now, he would walk through the door. She felt sick.

But Edward didn't come to the tea shop. He went into a bookseller.

"Are you waiting, miss?" A young girl in a black dress with a white apron stood by the table.

"Yes, thank you," mumbled Ellen.

"What would you like then, miss?"

Ellen went bright red.

"I mean I'm waiting for a, for a—" She didn't know what to say. Gentleman? No. Friend? No. Acquaintance. Perhaps that was the best thing to say. "I'm waiting for an acquaintance," she said.

"Of course, miss." The girl bobbed and went away.

Ellen stared at her gloved hands and tried to think of what she and Edward de Lacy could possibly talk about. Then, out of the corner of her eye, she saw him walk through the door and pretended to unbutton her gloves.

"Miss Spangle! How delightful to see you. May I sit down?" Edward took off his hat and smiled at her.

Ellen didn't know whether to apologise for Lucy's absence or make up some story to explain it. She heard her father's voice. *Never apologise, never explain, lass.*

Ellen smiled and indicated a chair. "I'm pleased to see you, too."

"I brought you a present." Edward handed her a packet wrapped in tissue. To his astonishment, he saw her face fall. "I'm sure you'll enjoy it," he said, almost plaintively.

"You are too kind, Mr. de Lacy," Ellen said. "But the truth is that I would prefer it if you stopped giving me presents."

She held the packet as if it was a bargaining card. "If I accept this, will you promise me it will be the last?"

"Didn't you approve of the little mirror I gave you?"

"It was exquisite," said Ellen. The moment she spoke, she wished she'd told him the truth. Now it was too late. "But I cannot accept anything further from you."

Edward bowed gravely. "Then I will obey your wishes."

"Thank you."

Ellen carefully unpeeled the layers of tissue paper and found herself staring at a calfskin-bound volume of Keats's poetry. She gasped. She had been studying these poems with Alfred Montmorency.

A shiver passed through her. Surely this man could not know Alfred Montmorency. He would have told her immediately. And of course it did not make sense. Alfred Montmorency knew her as Pearl Rowley. And he had promised to keep their arrangement confidential. It *must* be a coincidence.

Edward watched as a blush spread over Ellen's cream-coloured skin. He could have sworn her lips were trembling.

"Miss Spangle—," he began. "Uh, you see, Keats is one of my favourite poets." Edward paused and spoke as if half to himself. "'My heart aches, and a drowsy numbness pains my sense, as though of hemlock I had drunk.'" He smiled. "I believe 'Ode to a Nightingale' is his finest poem."

Ellen looked into Edward's eyes. They were clear. Nothing could hide in them. His choice of Keats *was* a coincidence. She ran her fingers over the smooth, gold-tooled leather. "Thank you. I can never explain how much this means to me."

Edward leaned forward and spoke quietly. "I would be honoured if you would try."

An hour later Lucy walked across Castle Square arm in arm with Joe Morgan. She held a drooping bunch of violets that he had given her.

"I don't understand," said Joe. "Why are we here?"

Joe Morgan was a stocky young man with an honest face and watchful eyes under dark brows. Lucy had fascinated him from the moment he saw her looking at his father's newly painted "zebras." He hadn't been able to resist teasing her about their wings, and even her ridiculous ignorance had enthralled him. Now she was peering into the crowded tea room with a sort of mischievous curiosity. Joe realised that something was going on he didn't know about.

"Why are you looking at your sister's acquaintance?"

"He's not an acquaintance," replied Lucy. "He's a gentleman admirer. But as you and me know, gentlemen live in a different world." She laughed. "My guess is he wanted to have tea with Sapphire Scarletta, not Ellen Spangle."

Joe nodded. There were always stories of gentlemen falling

in love with circus performers. None of the ones he knew had happy endings. "Did your mother agree to their meeting?"

"Oh, yes," said Lucy. Joe was so old-fashioned sometimes. Just like Ellen, now that she thought about it. "You see, Ellen is quite determined to leave the circus one day, and, well, she's very stubborn, so Mother felt it best to let her find out for herself."

"But your act is getting more and more popular," said Joe, frowning. It was the only thing about Lucy that made him feel uncomfortable. She must know that her father would have a fit if he found out they were meeting, and yet whenever he mentioned it, she tossed her head in the air and changed the subject, which left Joe to do all the worrying. "Has Ellen told your mother she wants to leave?"

Lucy shook her head. "If Mother ever found out Ellen was taking lessons from a tutor—"

"What?"

"She wants to be a teacher." Lucy scuffed her boot on the ground. "For someone who's so clever, Ellen can be very stupid."

Joe didn't understand. "There are lots of women teachers."

"Ellen's a circus performer," said Lucy sharply. "It's in her blood and she doesn't know it. That's why she's stupid."

Joe looked at the outline of Ellen's face through the window. He had never met her, but he had heard of her. Crush-Bone Ivan, his father's strong man, swore by her liniment, and her knack for training animals was well known. Now he could see that her expression was serious and thoughtful. Opposite her the young man was talking and waving his hands in the air.

"What are you staring at?"

There was something edgy in Lucy's voice.

Suddenly Joe understood that Lucy was supposed to be with her sister. Otherwise Norah Spangle would never have allowed such a meeting.

"Did you agree to be her chaperone?"

Lucy's eyes snapped open. "What if I did?" She pulled him away from the window and her face turned elfin and mischievous. "If I'd stayed with Ellen, how could I have seen you?"

Joe gazed into the emeralds that were Lucy's eyes. He watched as her lips shaped themselves into the tiniest pout, and he felt his insides tremble. He pushed away a vague feeling of behaving badly and slipped his arm through Lucy's.

What Ellen Spangle did with her life was none of his business.


Ellen met Edward for the next three Saturdays. He wooed her with stories. Soon she was dreaming of the tales of paintings and the faraway places he told her about, hour after hour, at Mrs. Hallward's Tea Room. In her dreams, she walked by the river in Paris and rocked in a gondola in Venice. She stood in the cool shade of St. Peter's Cathedral in Rome, away from the glare of the hot white streets. Ellen discovered that she loved listening to his stories. Little by little, in her dreams, Edward was at her side.

As for Edward, it was the stories he loved. Whether they

were true or not didn't mean anything to him. If he had never floated up the Grand Canal in a gondola or walked along the Seine, it didn't bother him. All he wanted was to see the look of rapture on Ellen's face.

One day, after describing how he had lived with a prince in a Moorish palace in southern Spain, he asked, "Will you tell me about the circus?"

It was what he wanted to know about more than anything else. It was the reason he had told her so many stories. He put his hands carefully in his lap, so she wouldn't see them trembling. "It must be so thrilling to hear hundreds of people clapping and cheering. And it's all because of you."

Ellen didn't know what to say.

She would have to explain that being a circus star was like being a freak. What was precious to her about their conversations was that they were about books and travel and paintings. But she knew he was curious, and since he had told her so much about himself, she knew it was only fair to tell him something of her life.

"It's a skill," said Ellen carefully. "I know it seems glamorous to the people watching. The truth is that it all depends on hard work and practice. That's all we do. Practice. Perform. Sleep." She looked away. "The applause is gratifying, I suppose. I hope I do my job well. But it's not one I want to do for the rest of my life."

"My father wants me to be a doctor," said Edward. "The sight of blood makes me faint."

"What will you do?"

"I shall paint," replied Edward. He smiled his beautiful, childlike smile. "Or perhaps I'll sit here forever and tell you stories."

Lucy's dreams changed too, as the weeks passed by. She dreamt of Joe Morgan. He was a tumbler and a clown in his father's circus, but Lucy knew he was a fine rider. She knew the bareback forward somersault would be a sensation if she did it with Ellen. But it would be a world-beating triumph if it was performed as a double act with a man. The more she thought about it, the more it took shape in her mind.

For the first time ever, it didn't matter to Lucy whether Ellen left Spangle's Circus. She had found her replacement in Joe. Nor did it matter to Lucy that she would be riding for Morgan's when she and Joe were together. What mattered to Lucy was fame and adulation. She didn't care how she got it.

Of course, neither Ellen nor Joe had any idea what Lucy was thinking, which suited her perfectly. Joe was obsessed with her, he would do what he was told. As for Ellen, she could take her chances.

Lucy would tell everyone her plans when the time was right.

# FIVE

"YOU TWO WILL JOIN THE BLEEDIN' ANGELS IF YOU CARRY ON like that!"

Fred Spangle stood at the open flap of the tent and watched Ellen and Lucy rehearse a new act. They began by standing on their horses with a handful of different-coloured ribbons. As Chestnut and Pearl cantered in opposite circles, Lucy and Ellen swapped ribbons. On the last circle they were supposed to jump onto the back of each other's horse as they passed one another. But each time they tried, Lucy jumped before Ellen was ready, so Pearl wound up with two riders while Chestnut cantered on her own around the ring.

As Fred watched, he became more and more angry. "Get down, the pair of you!" he roared, as if they were children.

Ellen slid down off Pearl's back. Lucy jumped down and glared at her father.

"Two days I've watched you!" shouted Fred. "And every time, it's a botched job!"

He turned to Lucy. "You nearly fell off last night, you stupid fool!" He whacked his leather boot with his whip.

"What good would you be with a broken leg?" He pushed his face close to hers. "No one wants to see a cripple in a fancy costume!"

Before Lucy could reply, Fred swung round to Ellen.

"And as for you. I'm sick to death of your moping face!" *Whack* went the cane against his boot. "Not a single smile during last night! Nor the night before! This ain't a convent! It's a circus ring!"

Ellen's cheeks were burning. It was hardly surprising that she and Lucy weren't working well together. They were arguing all the time. What's more, she knew perfectly well why the routine wasn't working, and she was as furious as her father. Time and time again she had tried to make Lucy wait, but the reason Lucy jumped too fast was because she wanted to be the one who was seen to jump first and get the applause. As each day passed, Ellen was more and more sickened by Lucy's selfishness and her own inability to make her see sense. She was beginning to hate Lucy, herself, and their whole routine.

Worst of all, no matter how hard Ellen tried to persuade her, Lucy refused to tell their mother about Joe Morgan. And since Norah believed that Lucy was Ellen's chaperone, that made Ellen into a liar as well.

"You ain't listenin'! You and your la-de-dah notions!" Fred grabbed Ellen's shoulder. "You're a circus performer, and don't you forget it!"

Ellen felt her temper soar.

"I'm *not* a circus performer, Father," she shouted. "I want—"

"I don't care what you *want*," yelled Fred. He raised his whip in the air.

"Stop it!" Norah strode across the ring and snatched the whip from Fred's hand. "I'll have no violence between you."

Something in Fred collapsed. His arms fell to his sides and he shook his head. "How could I have such a daughter?"

"Father!" cried Ellen. Her voice cracked in her throat. "Won't you listen this once?"

"*Listen?*" sneered Fred viciously. He grabbed back his whip and stamped away. "I don't *listen*. I run a circus."

That night Fred went to the pub with Ludwig. Norah knew he would come back drunk and Ludwig would be drunker. Ludwig was the only one who could calm Fred down when he got into one of his states. But Norah didn't care how drunk they were. She had something important to do, and she needed to be on her own.

Norah waited until the lights were out in the wagons around her. When she was almost positive Ellen and Lucy would be asleep, she wrapped her shawl around her shoulders and walked over to their lodgings.

As she had expected, Ellen woke up the moment Norah opened the door.

"Who's there?"

"Shhh, Ellen, it's Ma." Norah took Ellen's coat from its hook on the wall and crept across the room.

"Is the lion sick?"

"No."

Ellen felt the rough wool of her coat being pushed into her hands.

"Hurry," whispered Norah. "Don't wake Lucy."

Ellen slid out of bed and pushed her feet into her worn black boots. If she needed her coat, she would need her boots, too. She closed the door behind her and followed her mother across Fender's Field.

It was warm in her parents' wagon. Norah had banked up the stove. Now she lit the paraffin lamp and put the kettle on to boil.

Ellen sat in the corner of a wooden bench with her heavy coat wrapped around her knees. The smells of the wagon brought back her childhood: smoky paraffin, musty animal hair, and the faintest whiff of lavender. Her mother stuffed dried bunches of it between the blankets to keep away fleas.

Ellen watched sleepily as Norah measured out two teaspoons of tea and poured the boiling water into the teapot. Ellen remembered drinking tea made from burnt toast when times were hard. Now, as she saw her mother break off a hefty lump of sugar and divide it between their two cups, she knew there was something important on her mind. It was always the same with Norah. The more difficult the problem, the sweeter the tea.

"It's Edward, isn't it?" said Ellen quietly.

Norah looked up. "Yes." She poured out Ellen's tea and stirred it so the sugar would dissolve. "I made a mistake, Ellen. I should never have let Lucy come with you."

Ellen was so taken aback, she said nothing.

"I'm not worried about you," said Norah carefully. "You will do the right thing. Lucy is different. I can't trust her." Norah paused. "I'm afraid the company of your gentleman has given her ideas above her station."

Ellen heard her mother's words through a fog. She felt entirely desperate. She couldn't deny it, because then she would have to betray Lucy. But she knew that once her mother got a notion in her head, it was almost impossible to make her change her mind.

"Mother—," she began. She stopped. She didn't know what to say.

Norah held up her hand. "Hear me out, Ellen. I'm sure your Mr. de Lacy is a gentleman. What I'm saying is that Lucy has an envious cast of mind. Something is going on with her. And I don't like it."

Ellen's head felt hot and achy.

Lucy. Lucy. Lucy.

It was always the same, and Ellen was sick of it.

Did it not occur to her mother that the relationship between her and Edward might have changed? They had been seeing each other for a month now. Had her mother not noticed they had become more than acquaintances?

Ellen put down her cup of tea. Sugar or no sugar, it tasted bitter as burnt toast.

"You're making a mistake."

"No, Ellen. I am not." Norah put down her own tea. "I want you to stop seeing Mr. de Lacy. For your own good as well as Lucy's."

Ellen stared at her mother's almost mannish features. It was her black eyes that made her face striking. They missed nothing. Ellen hated lying. It was time to tell her mother as much of the truth as she could.

"My meetings with Edward de Lacy have not turned *my* head," she said in a cold voice. "Unless by that you mean it is wrong to find another person's conversation interesting." She unclenched her fists and spread her fingers in her lap. "My life is not with the circus, Mother. I intend to leave as soon as I can find suitable employment."

The wagon was silent as a grave.

"Does your father know this?"

Anger shot up through Ellen's body like a fire-tipped arrow.

"For heaven's sake, Mother. I have tried to tell both of you as much for over a year now. Neither of you will listen."

"Perhaps we have listened ... but we know you are making a mistake," said Norah quietly.

But Ellen wasn't hearing her. "Don't you care about me at all, Mother?" she cried. "Don't you want to know *why* I want to leave?"

Norah rubbed her hands over her face. "You are the only

one in my family I can rely on," she said wearily. "Your father is hot-blooded and showy. Lucy is all that and unreliable." She shrugged. "Sam is too young. What do you want me to say?"

"I want you to respect my right to lead my own life as I want," said Ellen bitterly. She refused to let her mother make her feel guilty. Why should she? "I'm not my sister's keeper."

"Your father told me it would come to this," Norah said, half to herself. "Your lessons would—"

"Give me ideas above my station?" interrupted Ellen furiously. She glared at her mother. "Perhaps Lucy and I have the same problem after all."

"Ellen, please!" cried Norah hopelessly. "Have you forgotten it was me that had you all learn to read and write?"

Ellen looked into her mother's face. It was grey and sad and tired. She loved her mother desperately. The last thing she wanted was to add to her problems.

"I'm sixteen, Mother," said Ellen. "I can make my own decisions."

"So you won't stop seeing Mr. de Lacy?"

"No. But at least you will know the truth."

"The truth," repeated Norah. She shook her head. "What *is* the truth?"

Ellen knew her mother was thinking of Lucy. And she was worried sick. Despair and confusion washed over Ellen. She threw her arms around her mother's shoulders and sobbed.

Norah held her daughter and felt the secrets that struggled in her mind. She stared at the sooty flame of the paraffin lamp and prayed that when trouble came it would not be too bad.

Ellen couldn't wait any longer. Ever since she had crept back from her mother's wagon, she had lain in the dark beside Lucy and rehearsed what she was going to say to her. Now she gently shook her sister's warm shoulders. "Lucy! Wake up!"

Lucy groaned and opened her eyes. A faint pink light wobbled around the edge of the curtain. It was barely dawn.

"It's too early," she muttered. "Leave me alone. Let me sleep."

"Wake up. I have to talk to you."

"Can't it wait?"

All Ellen's hopes of being reasonable and patient disappeared. "No, it can't wait, because it's all your bloody fault."

Lucy sat up with a jerk. "What are you talking about?"

"I won't be a liar just because you are," cried Ellen. "You've got to tell them about Joe, Lucy. Or someone else will."

"How?" snapped Lucy. "No one knows but you."

"Don't be so stupid," said Ellen. "Someone's bound to have seen you together. People talk. For all I know, someone told Father last night at the pub."

Lucy's face went white. This was not how she had planned things.

"Father'd go crazy if he found out about Joe," she whispered. "He'd stop me seeing him."

"He won't like it," said Ellen coldly. "But he'll get over it."

"He won't like it because he depends on me for everything!" Lucy's eyes flared like torches. "Because you're so bloody cracked."

"*Cracked?*" cried Ellen. "What do you mean, *cracked?*"

"For such a bookworm, you really are *stupid*," said Lucy. "Can't you see that a moon-faced sissy like Edward would never stick by you? You're a circus girl. He's a gentleman." Lucy spoke as if she was talking to a moron. "His fancy parents would never have it."

Ellen was so stung she blurted out what she had sworn to keep secret. "He loves me," she cried. "He says when he's twenty-one, he will have his own fortune. We will be free to do what we like."

"And you believe him?"

"Of course I believe him!" cried Ellen. "Not everyone is a dirty little liar like you."

Lucy reached out to yank Ellen's hair, but Ellen saw her coming and held her wrist tightly in her hand.

"Let go," shrieked Lucy. "You're hurting me!"

"Promise you'll tell Father and Mother about Joe Morgan," shouted Ellen.

"I'll tell them about your lessons!"

"I don't care! At least we'll all know the truth."

"Oooh, the truth," sneered Lucy. "That's all you care about." She pulled back her hand and Ellen let her go. "You're such a *fool*."

§ § §

Ellen sat in a cold, filthy doorway and wrapped her shawl tightly around her shoulders. Even though it was just dawn, the street sellers and hawkers were already arguing over their pitches and setting up their barrows for the day. A smell of fried fish and hot meat puddings hung in the air. Ellen realised she was hungry. And the hungrier she felt, the angrier she became with Lucy. She would have been eating breakfast with their mother now if she hadn't walked out. But she was so disgusted with her sister after their argument that the idea of sharing a bed was intolerable. So she had put on her clothes and left.

"Mind if I sit with ya?" A young man with lank orange hair slumped down beside her. He wore a blue coachman's greatcoat and carried an old leather suitcase in his hands.

Ellen reluctantly shifted to make room in the doorway.

"Don't worry, miss, I ain't goin' to bovver ya."

The young man pointed to his suitcase. "Only I didn't want to carry them around much longer. There's a bit of a wait till the street fills up." As he spoke he covered the suitcase with his heavy coat.

Despite herself, Ellen was curious. And now that she knew he wasn't a bother, her curiosity made her feel better. "What's in your suitcase?"

"Snakes."

The young man had a freckled face and pale, gummy eyes. He reached into his pocket and unwrapped a parcel of greasy paper. Inside were two ends of a loaf and some dripping. "'Ave some. You look 'ungry."

"I am."

His kindness brought a lump to Ellen's throat. She turned her head away so he couldn't see her face.

"Go on, then." He held out the bread again.

This time, Ellen took a piece. "What kind of snakes?" she asked, wiping her nose with her sleeve.

"Smallish ones," replied the young man. He bit into his own bread. "You see, I swallows 'em for a penny, so I wouldn't want 'em too big, would I?" His eyes were serious, as if he was explaining a dilemma to a child.

Ellen laughed suddenly and spattered her skirt with her mouthful of bread.

The young man grinned. "See, that's better, ain't it? 'Ave a bit more."

As Ellen chewed on her bread, she saw a girl called Ada across the street. Ada waved and Ellen waved back. Ada was a tough, skinny Northerner who sold the best pea soup in London, thick as porridge and twice as tasty.

"She a friend of yours?" asked the young man.

"Sort of, I suppose," said Ellen. "I've known her for years, but we've never said much."

"She's my sister," said the young man. "We keeps an eye on each other." He looked across the street to where Ada was doling out soup in farthing twists of greasy paper. "Blood's thicker than water, Ada says."

"What's your name?"

"Adam." He tapped the suitcase. "Adam and Eve. Garden of Eden. Good name for a snake swallower, Ada says."

"Is it your real name?"

Adam shrugged. "Ada gave it to me. She's my only family." He ripped off another piece of bread. "Ada can read the Bible."

There was a Spangle family Bible. Norah kept it by her bed. It had been given to her father by his mother. On the inside pages all the births and deaths that had happened in the past fifty years were set down in different handwritings. It occurred to Ellen that her mother was probably the first Spangle woman who could write in the names herself.

"Ada told me about you," said Adam. "Must be a good life working in a circus." He stared at Ellen curiously. "Better than walking the streets and swallowing snakes."

"What's it like swallowing a snake?" Ellen asked quickly. The last thing she wanted to talk about was the circus.

Adam thought for a moment. "First you gotta remember to 'old on to their tail," he said. "Otherwise, they'd be down yer throat like a rat down a pipe."

Ellen shuddered, and Adam laughed. "That's what they all do when I tells 'em!"

"What does it feel like?"

"Queer taste," said Adam thoughtfully. "And rough. Not when they go in, o' course. They're smooth an' they sort of curl up." He threw his head back and pretended to pull out a snake. "It's when they come out, with their scales all backwards."

Ellen put down her bread. "Doesn't it hurt?"

"Yus," said Adam. "But Ada gives me this linctus." He stared at Ellen. "Fact is, she says you makes it and gives it to her free."

"Not free," said Ellen. Ada was proud like the rest of the street sellers. "I swap it for soup."

"Lucky for me, then," said Adam. "'Cos nothing else works." He looked sideways at her. "Feeling better now?"

Ellen felt her cheeks redden. "Why do you ask?"

"'Cos Ada sent me," said Adam. "She saw you sitting here. 'Not herself, Adam,' she said. 'You stay wiv her till she's better.'" He nodded to where his sister was dishing out soup to a crowd of people holding up their money. "Now's her busy time. She couldn't get away herself."

Adam stood up and dusted down his thick blue coat. The suitcase of snakes sat on the steps between them. "I'd show you, 'cept they catch cold real easy."

"Yes, I know."

"O' course you would, working in a circus." Adam shifted awkwardly from foot to foot.

Ellen got to her feet. "Thank you. Tell Ada, won't you?"

Adam nodded and shuffled into the crowded street with his suitcase.

Ellen felt a penny in her pocket. It was just enough to buy a slice of Lucy's favourite plum dough cake.

Ada was right. Blood was thicker than water.

# SIX

"GAWD SAVE US, ELLEN! I'VE BEEN LOOKING FOR YOU EVERY-where!" cried Fred Spangle desperately. Ellen knew he had completely forgotten what had happened between them in the ring.

"What's wrong, Father?"

"Everything's wrong," cried Fred. "Everything's bleedin' wrong since that bleedin' mirror broke."

"Where's Mother?"

"She's sick under her blankets. Bad oyster. Anyway, it's not 'er I'm worried about. It's Claudius." He stared at Ellen with wild red eyes. "'E's in a bad way, Ellen. Worse than I ever seen him."

"Where's Ludwig?" Ellen felt the plum dough cake in her pocket. She wanted to find Lucy before she settled into one of her terrible sulks. "He's seen to Claudius before."

"Ludwig's passed out cold," mumbled Fred. He stared at his hands as if they weren't part of him. "Bit of a night, it was." Suddenly he buried his head in his hands and wept. "If we lose Claudius—"

Ellen understood now that her father was still drunk.

"Father. Listen to me. I've never physicked Claudius."

"Gawd help me, Ellen!" Fred's voice rose. "Your mother's sick! Ludwig's flat out! I don't know what to do!"

"Stop shouting," said Ellen in a weary voice. "I'll do the best that I can. But if he dies, don't blame me." She dug into her pocket and held out the plum cake. "Promise you'll give this to Lucy for me."

"Lucy's not 'ere," muttered Fred. "Little hussy ran off this morning without a by-your-leave." Suddenly his eyes narrowed as if he had just remembered something that had made him really angry. "Last night—"

Ellen turned and ran.


Ellen climbed up the steps to Claudius's cage and peered through the bars. The stink was suffocating. The lion lay on his side with his head thrown slightly back. He was breathing in short, shallow snatches. No wonder Fred had been worried. Ellen opened the cage door and slid in beside him. She knew he was too sick to be dangerous. His body was hot and his fur felt thin and stringy. She put her hand carefully on his shoulders. All the muscles were slack.

"Jesus Christ, Ellen!" hissed a voice. "Are you barmy? Get out of there."

Ellen looked up to see Jake's horrified face on the other side of the bars.

"He's sick," whispered Ellen.

"He's dying," said the juggler. "Now get out of there or I'll pull you out."

Ellen crawled backwards out of the cage and carefully shut the door.

"I think it's pneumonia."

"Whatever he's got, he's a goner," said Jake.

"No, he's not," replied Ellen angrily. "If it was you, a doctor would make a poultice to bring out the fever."

Jake looked at her as if she was crazy. "He's a lion."

"I don't care," snapped Ellen. "I'm going to try it."

"It might kill him quicker," said Jake.

Ellen looked into Jake's sharp red eyes. "I promised Father I'd try."

"You look like you didn't sleep last night," said Jake gently.

"I didn't."

Jake didn't have to ask why. The whole circus knew Lucy and Ellen weren't getting on.

"All right," said Jake finally. "What do you want me to do?"

Two hours later Claudius was trussed up so he couldn't move. Jake had built a low fire under his cage to help him sweat out the fever. Ellen had rubbed a poultice of powdered mustard and oil of turpentine into his chest and wrapped him round with oilcloth. Then they drilled holes in the wooden wall by his head so he could breathe more easily. When they had finished, Claudius looked like a greasy parcel with a head and tail sticking out either end. Now all they could do was wait.

"You get a rest," said Jake. "You'll need it before tonight."

Ellen shook her head. "I have to watch him myself."

"I'll watch him."

But Ellen didn't reply. She covered herself in a warm blanket and huddled on the top steps of the cage. "Tell my mother what I've done," she said. She rubbed her hand across her face. "And tell her to keep Father away."

Jake looked puzzled but left her alone.

A few minutes later, she slumped sideways.

When Jake was sure she was asleep, he picked her up, still wrapped in her blanket, and carried her across to Norah's wagon.

It was barely midday.


Ellen woke up to the smell of frying kidneys. Her mother sat in the corner of the wagon. Ellen eased herself up on her elbow. "Feeling better?"

Norah nodded ruefully. "But no good when I was needed."

Ellen's stomach went hollow. "Is he dead?"

"We'll know tomorrow." Norah tipped a pan of kidneys and gravy onto a bowl and handed it over with a piece of bread.

Ellen thought of Claudius wrapped up in his stinking oilcloth parcel. "I didn't know what else to do with him, Ma."

"I would have done the same."

Ellen mopped up a mouthful of rich brown gravy. It was only as she finished the second mouthful that she remembered Lucy. "Has Lucy come back?"

Norah nodded. "She's in one of her sulks, I'm afraid."

Ellen wiped her bowl clean with the last of her bread and pushed away the blanket. She had to find Lucy before their show that night.

"Will you look in on Claudius?" asked Ellen.

Norah nodded. "I'll take care of him now."

Ellen stared into her mother's dark eyes. She was sure she knew about her argument with Lucy. Suddenly the air was heavy between them.

Norah took the empty bowl from Ellen's hand.

"Drink your tea before it gets cold."

"Ladies and gemmen! The Greatest Show on Earth! The Wonders of the Jungle! The Incredible Scarletta Sisters! Julius Jake the Juggling King! Tonight and only tonight. Don't miss your chance. Step up! Step up!"

Sam stood on top of a barrel on the steps of the theatre and bawled as loud as he could in a high-pitched voice. A large crowd was gathering. He took a deep breath and started his patter all over again.

"Ladies and gemmen," squeaked Sam. "The Greatest Show—" At that moment, he saw Ellen on her way to her lodgings. He jumped down and chased after her.

"Jake said you saved Claudius!" Sam wrapped his arms

around his sister's waist. "Jake said he carried you to Mother's wagon."

"I was wondering who took me," said Ellen. "I thought it might have been Father."

Sam shook his head. "Father's been yelling at Lucy all afternoon and she's been yelling back." He pulled a face. "I'm surprised they didn't wake you."

Ellen's heart sank as she thought of her father's final drunken words. "What were they fighting about?"

"Father told Lucy that she wasn't as good as she thought she was. Then Lucy—" Sam's face crumpled.

"What happened?"

Tears welled up in Sam's eyes. "Lucy hit Pa across the face with her riding whip."

"Dear God! Did he hit her back?"

"She ran off before he could do anything." Sam wiped his nose with his sleeve. "I haven't seen her since."

"When was that?"

Sam shrugged. "In the afternoon, sometime."

Ellen put her arms around her brother's shoulders. "You get on with your patter. Don't worry about Pa and Lucy. Everyone's bad. It's been a long winter. Everything will be all right, you'll see."

But she knew she was lying. And Sam knew it too.

"Lots of people on the streets," said Sam quickly. "We're going to be full."

"Then I'd better shift my stumps and change."

ၐ  ၐ  ၐ

Lucy peered at herself in the mirror and drew a thick black line around her eyelids. She scooped up a blob of cochineal paste on the end of her forefinger and outlined her lips. Then she smudged some powdered green pigment on the lids of her eyes.

Lucy had never worn makeup in the ring before. Her mother had always forbidden it. Now she looked at her reflection in the mirror. Her red satin jacket and frothy, sequined net skirt made her look like a fairy queen. Her painted face made her look disturbing and exotic. Lucy grinned to herself and twirled around the room.

At that moment Ellen walked in. She stopped and stared.

"Don't say anything!" cried Lucy gaily. "It's only tonight!" She twirled past Ellen. "Don't you think I look wonderful?"

Ellen thought she looked dreadful, but she wasn't about to say so. She had come to make peace between them.

"Lucy," she began.

"No!" cried Lucy. "No! No! No! I shall not hear a word of it. You were right to be cross with me." Her voice was high and brittle. "Anyway, it's different now!"

"What do you mean, *different*?"

Lucy pulled up the wooden chair and arranged her skirts so they wouldn't be crushed when she sat down. "It's different because I had a row with Father, and so now I'm engaged to Joe." She felt for a loose curl and pinned it back into place. "Joe's coming tonight. We'll tell Father afterwards."

She grabbed Ellen's hands and pulled them onto her lap.

"Father was so horrible to me, I couldn't wait any longer."

Ellen's mind spun like a top. It took every ounce of her will not to scream at her sister. How could she come to an arrangement with Joe without even asking their parents? But Ellen was desperate not to argue with Lucy again. She forced herself to try to see something good in what was about to happen.

"People say Joe's nothing like Jeremiah," she said at last. "I'm sure Father will agree to your engagement."

Lucy's painted eyes glittered. "He won't have to."

Ellen went cold. Lucy didn't need to say any more. She was deserting her family.

"Oh, Lucy," whispered Ellen. "What have you done?"

Lucy threw back Ellen's hands with such force they hit Ellen's face before she could stop them.

"I haven't *done* anything!" she screamed. She grabbed her shawl and pushed her feet into her boots. "But when I do, I'll do what I *want*!" She pushed her face in front of Ellen's. "I'm not propping you up any longer! I want a life of my own!"

She stamped out of the room and slammed the door behind her.


Sam was right. They had a full house. And tonight, it was a good crowd. They were excited and happy. If they shut up and watched, they were on your side. If they hollered and yelled all the way through, the show was a warm-up for a night in the pub.

After Lucy had run off, Ellen had quickly changed and gone to look for her. She went to the stables, where they always checked their horses one last time. She went to her mother's wagon. She even went down to Claudius's cage to see if Lucy might be there. She couldn't find her anywhere. Now she stood in the back room behind the ring and heard the trombones sputtering. The clowns' tumbling act was almost over. There was about a minute to go before she and Lucy were on.

"Ladies and gemmen!" boomed Fred Spangle in his rich, velvety voice. "All the way from the palaces of Italy—the wonder of kings, the pride of princes—*The Amazing Scarletta Sisters*!"

The drums rolled. The bandsmen played their special music. Ellen watched in a daze as two boys in silver jackets led Pearl and Chestnut into the ring.

Ellen stood rooted to the spot. She didn't know what to do.

"Ladies and gemmen," cried Fred again, smoothly hiding the surprise in his voice.

Suddenly there was a great roar of applause. Ellen stepped forward and watched in disbelief as Lucy rushed in from the other side of the ring. She bowed and jumped onto Chestnut's back. She stood up and held her hands in the air. The crowd roared.

Ellen was dumbfounded. They hadn't rehearsed anything different for tonight. What on Earth was going on?

Fred turned. He was just as confused as Ellen, but he

knew he had to get them both into the ring as fast as possible. Now that Lucy was behaving so strangely, anything could happen. And only Ellen would be able to put a stop to it.

Fred's voice rang out. "Ladies and gemmen! I give you ... Seraphina Scarletta! And a round of applause for her sister, the incredible Sapphire!"

With legs that didn't feel like hers, Ellen ran into the hot, blazing theatre. "Watch her!" hissed Fred as Ellen passed him. She nodded to show him she'd heard, then leapt onto Pearl's back.

Lucy stayed standing and threw out an arm as if in welcome. Ellen's blood ran cold. She was definitely up to something, but what? Their first routine was a seated gallop through hoops. A great white smile flashed across Lucy's painted face. "We're doing the ribbons!" she yelled as she cantered past. "I'll show the bastard I can ride!" Then she shoved a bunch of yellow ribbons into her sister's hands. Ellen's heart hammered in her chest. So this was Lucy's plan. In rehearsals, they had only managed to switch horses smoothly the one time. She turned Pearl round and tried to canter alongside Lucy. It was madness to do the ribbon routine. But Lucy whooped and wheeled her horse round. Now they were cantering in opposite directions. It was the beginning of their act. Ellen knew it was too late to stop her.

The crowd roared and stamped their feet. There was

something exciting and furious in Seraphina's face they had never seen before and they loved it.

Ellen stood up on Pearl's back and gripped the horse's haunches with the insides of her leather-soled slippers. The sticky resin dust held her feet in position. All she could do was watch Lucy's every movement and grab her reins if she had to.

Now Lucy was cantering towards her, the ribbons held high in her right hand. They passed within inches of each other and swapped over ribbons. At each handover they whooped and shouted. For Ellen, it was what they had rehearsed. For Lucy, it sounded like a war cry. By the sixth time round, Ellen had all the red ribbons and Lucy had all the yellow ones.

It was time for the jump to change horses.

After the problems they had with timing, they decided that Lucy would throw her ribbons on the ground. Then Ellen would do the same. When they had completed a full circle without the ribbons, they would jump and switch horses. It seemed the best way to synchronize their timing, and in rehearsal it had worked well.

Now Ellen waited for Lucy to throw her ribbons down, but she didn't. Instead she galloped past and snatched the ones in Ellen's hand.

The crowd roared. Ellen knew she had seconds to decide what to do. If she chased her sister around the ring and made a grab for her reins, the crowd would know immediately that something was wrong. And that was unthinkable. Everyone would demand their money back and Fred would be furious. Yet if she sat back and did nothing, who knew what crazy stunt Lucy might try to pull? She caught her father's eye to ask for help. Fred made a twirling motion with his crooked finger. He was telling her to get out of the ring.

Now everyone was looking at Lucy. She knew they adored her. A smile flashed across her face. Lucy had no words to describe how she felt. She was a sensation. She was invincible.

She stared down at her sequined skirt as she cantered round and round the ring. The sequins glittered in the light of the chandelier. She waved the red and yellow ribbons in the air as if they were flames dancing about her head. Then she threw them aside and urged Chestnut forward.

The theatre fell silent. There was no noise except for the hiss of the gas jets and the thud of Chestnut's hooves. Everyone knew something extraordinary was going to happen.

Lucy felt her mind fill with light. She imagined power blazing through her body. She stepped back on Chestnut's haunches.

Suddenly Ellen knew what Lucy was planning, and her head filled with one long, terrible scream. It was what she had promised never to try. Even Fred had admitted he had been wrong to encourage her. Now Ellen watched in absolute horror as Lucy threw herself into a forward somersault.

It was a pure, smooth, beautiful movement. Lucy curled herself into a ball and spun upwards with the momentum of her jump. Chestnut cantered evenly beneath her. Each stride was exactly the length of the one before.

Then Chestnut stumbled and Lucy soared over her neck.

As Ellen watched, everything happened very slowly. She saw Lucy hit the ground with a soft thud. But they had both been taught how to fall. Lucy would know that by rolling very slightly forward, the back of her shoulders would cushion the impact of the fall. Ellen waited for her sister to roll. Nothing happened. For a second, she wondered whether Lucy was playing her crowd to the hilt.

The crowd in the tent was silent. Then Chestnut cantered around the ring and jumped carefully over Lucy's body, and Ellen knew her sister was dead.

Fred Spangle curled back his whip and snapped it. The *crack* cut through Ellen's mind and made every nerve in her body twang.

"Ladies and gemmen! Miss Sapphire Scarletta!" Fred cracked his whip again to make sure Ellen understood. But it wasn't necessary. Ellen knew what she had to do. It was a full house.

She cantered back into the ring.

Fred signalled to the band and they played a tune Ellen recognised immediately. It was an old routine she did with Lucy. Only this time, there was no Lucy beside her. She set off, her arms in the air, her head thrown back, with a smile on her face. Out of the corner of her eye, she saw Ludwig and a clown run into the ring. Ludwig was wearing his black and green embroidered vest with a pair of boxing gloves hung from his waist. As Ellen cantered past, they covered Lucy in a scarlet cloak and carried her quickly out of the ring.

"Ladies and gemmen!" cried Fred. His voice was smooth and reassuring, as if he had good news to tell. "Miss Seraphina Scarletta is unhurt. Forgive the interruption."

There was a ragged cheer from the crowd.

*It was all part of the act! Hadn't they all noticed how she had rolled to one side to break her fall? Yes, of course they had. What a blessing! Thank the Lord for his mercy!*

The music stopped. Ellen rode out of the ring, blinded by tears.

Lucy lay on her side on the wooden table in the back room behind the stage. Her slippered feet were tucked up underneath her frothy, sequined skirt. With her painted red lips, she looked like a doll waiting to be wrapped in tissue paper.

Norah cupped Lucy's head in her hands. "Silly girl," she whispered. "Why'd you have to go and do that?" Then she slumped down on her knees and pressed her face against the mass of Lucy's bright red hair.

Ellen touched her sister's cheek. It was warm, and there was a faintly surprised look on her face.

A few feet away, in another world, there was a roar of laughter. *Lord Rowley! Lord Rowley!*

Fred Spangle came into the room. His charcoal-lined

eyebrows and rouged cheeks made him look like something from a nightmare. His lips pulled and twisted on his face.

"Where's Sam?" he muttered.

"Out the front with the takings," said Norah. She slowly got to her feet.

"Better tell him, lass," said Fred.

Norah nodded but didn't move. She couldn't bear to leave Lucy, because she knew she was leaving her forever.

Fred put his hands on Lucy's shoulders and turned her round. Then he gently straightened her arms and legs.

He turned to Norah and Ellen. His eyes were two red holes. "She'll not fit into her box else," he whispered.

# SEVEN

A WEEK LATER ELLEN SAT WITH EDWARD BY THE RIVER. AS SHE told him what had happened, her voice seemed to belong to somebody else.

Edward trembled as he listened. "What happened to Claudius?"

"His fever left him," said Ellen in a dull voice. It seemed odd that Edward would ask after the lion first, but she didn't care. "He'll live. My mother is looking after him now."

The truth was that Ellen often found her mother in the sick lion's cage, stroking his head and staring at the wall. She couldn't bear to tell Edward that Norah had abandoned Sam.

"I can't comfort him, Ellen," Norah had said. "I can't even look at him." Her face twisted as she fought to control her voice. "You see, I'm afraid I'll lose him, too."

They both knew what she was saying didn't make any sense, but then nothing made sense anymore.

So it had fallen to Ellen to look after Sam. She made sure he went to his lessons and did what work was given to him. She made sure that he washed and that he ate his supper at night. In the end, Sam came to share her room. At least that way, Ellen knew he wasn't sleeping in his clothes.

Fred swung from rage to despair to rage again. He stomped around Fender's Field, shouting at whoever crossed his path. A few days after Lucy's death, Sam tried to cheer his father up by painting a donkey with stripes to look like a zebra. It was the sort of trick that always made Fred laugh, but Sam didn't remember it was a trick Jeremiah Morgan had played last summer.

Fred cuffed Sam's ear and whacked the donkey with his whip.

"You stupid eejit," he bellowed. "Ain't you got something useful to do?"

Ellen had watched Sam creep away like a kicked dog, leading the donkey behind him. She tried not to feel angry at her father, but it was almost impossible. All of them were suffering. Why did he have to make things worse?

As for Ellen, she moved through her days like a sleepwalker. At night she woke with Lucy's voice calling her: *Ellen! Ellen!*

Twice Ellen had jumped out of bed. Another time she had run to the door and yanked it open. "Yes! Yes! Lucy, I'm here!" Then, after a couple of seconds, the cold, sickening knowledge that Lucy was dead and she would never see her again cut through her body like a knife.

And the pain seemed to get worse, not better. Ellen missed her Lucy more than she could have imagined possible. Every day she cursed herself for not guessing that Lucy would try the forward somersault. As the days passed, Ellen forgot the disagreements she had had with her sister. Instead she felt the touch of Lucy's hands on her hair as she drew it back and rolled it into a bun at the back of her neck. She heard Lucy's crow of delight as she tried on a new second-hand outfit and spun like a fairy on a musical box in the middle of their cramped, dark room. Even the room seemed darker and dingier. Sometimes Ellen opened Lucy's clothes chest and took out a skirt and a jacket and a blouse and fitted them all together. Then she sat on their one saggy chair with Lucy's skirt draped over her knees and Lucy's jacket lying against her shoulders and she wept.

One day Sam came in and saw her. He stood without moving, and the look of terror on his face made Ellen understand that she was losing a grip on her own sanity.

"Please," begged Sam. "Promise me you'll never do that again." And Ellen stood up and let Lucy's clothes fall on the floor.

"I promise," she whispered. She held Sam in her arms for what seemed like hours.


Now Ellen watched the barges sailing down the Thames. It was low tide, and stringy, mud-slicked children were poking down into the riverbank with long poles. Mudlarks, they called them. Each one believed they would find a purse of sovereigns one day. It was the only thing that kept them alive, even though most of them never lived long enough to find more than a dozen coppers and a fob watch or two.

Slowly Ellen became aware that Edward was agitated. He had not spoken for a while, and his knuckles were white where his hands gripped the seat.

"I'm sorry," she mumbled. "I didn't mean to upset you."

"It is me who is sorry, my dearest. I cannot bear to see you so sad." Edward's eyes glittered as if behind a film of tears. "I wish, I only wish—"

"What?" Ellen bowed her head.

"If only I had been with you. I might have helped somehow."

"No one could have helped," said Ellen. "Father sent us all away. That night the carpenters built a coffin. She was buried the next day."

"Surely there was a service?"

"Tower Hamlets is a public cemetery," said Ellen quietly. "Father doesn't hold with God much."

"But a parson came?"

"Yes. A parson came."

Edward squeezed Ellen's hand. "We shall put flowers on her grave."

Ellen was about to say no. There had been no flowers at the graveside except for Sam's bunch of squashed violets. Suddenly the violets made her think of Joe Morgan. Lucy always brought back the violets he gave her and put them in a vase in their room. The thought of Joe made Ellen feel even more miserable. In the shock after Lucy's death she'd forgotten he had been in the crowd that night, let alone their planned announcement to Fred. Tears welled up again. The chances were Joe wouldn't even know where Lucy was buried. Joe was said to be a kind, honest young man. And still she didn't have the courage to go and find him. Ellen slumped against Edward's shoulder.

Edward pressed his lips against Ellen's hair. It smelled of coal tar and lemons and reminded him of his nursery. It was his favourite smell. As Ellen wept quietly, Edward's heart swelled in his chest. This beautiful young woman was his own true love. She was the biggest and best secret in his life. He adored her.

"Come," whispered Edward. He knew she was crying at the thought of Lucy's neglected grave. "We'll take Lucy flowers. She'll like that."

An hour later Ellen waited by the huge iron gate to Tower Hamlets cemetery while Edward went to get flowers. It never occurred to Ellen to ask what flowers he would buy. She imagined a bunch of green and white hellebores and some early daffodils. Even a bunch of violets.

Edward's voice was proud and excited. "I found some at last!" He was holding a huge bunch of red roses.

Ellen stared at the flowers, and bile rushed upwards into her throat. Lucy had hated the red roses from the moment she knew they weren't for her. How could Edward be so thoughtless and stupid?

Fury surged through Ellen's body. "No! No! No!" she screamed. She grabbed the roses from Edward's hands. The thorns ripped her hand and made her fingers bleed.

She threw the flowers on the ground and stamped them into the mud. Hard, rasping sobs shook her body. As she grabbed the iron gate to stop herself from falling, she saw her own blood dripping down through her fingers. She slumped to the ground and howled.

Edward stared at her in horror. He couldn't understand what he had done wrong. He had chosen the roses especially. Lucy had been a star. She was Seraphina Scarletta. You always gave red roses to a star. Edward had been sure that Ellen would praise him for his generosity and for including Lucy in the tribute he had always paid to her.

"Ellen!" he stuttered. He reached for her hand, but she pulled it away.

"Don't say anything," cried Ellen in a choked voice. "You don't understand! You don't understand!" She got to her feet and straightened her skirt. "I'm going home."

"Let me come with you," cried Edward desperately.

Neither of them looked at the wrecked flowers at their feet.

Ellen shook her head. "No, I'll go alone. It's better that way."

"But when will I see you again?" asked Edward. He was almost crying.

Ellen felt more and more confused. It was almost as if his sister had died, not hers.

"Please!" cried Edward. "At least let me come to Fender's Field and see you!"

"No!" said Ellen again. "It's too soon." She pushed back a few strands of damp hair from her face and tried to wipe some of the sticky blood from her hands with her handkerchief. The sight of her own blood helped her think more clearly. It was not the time for outsiders to come anywhere near the family. And Edward's red roses had shaken her horribly. "My mother and father are not themselves."

"I *have* to see you!"

Again, Ellen heard something in Edward's voice she didn't understand. Surely he had his paintings to finish. He had mentioned an exhibition in the spring. "Perhaps in a fortnight," she said at last.

"Will you stop riding?"

For a moment Ellen was so taken aback by his question, she didn't know what to say.

"What do you mean?" she asked finally.

Edward stared at his feet and his face went bright red. "The circus," he mumbled. "I was—"

Ellen felt a dizziness wash over her. She couldn't believe what she was hearing. She gazed down at the ruined red petals spread over the road. "Are you asking me if I will stop working?"

Ellen looked into Edward's face, but he had turned away and wouldn't meet her eyes. "Why on Earth would you want to know that?"

"I—I—was thinking about your strength, dearest," said Edward uncomfortably. Ellen knew he was lying.

"Of course I must ride," replied Ellen. "What else can I do?" The dizziness turned into hopelessness.

Edward took her hands in his. "Please forgive me. Of course, I'll wait until you are ready to see me."

Ellen looked up into Edward's face once more. He was such a child in many ways, and she loved him for his innocence and enthusiasm. But for the first time, she felt uneasy. She pushed the thought away because it worried her too much. "I forgive you," she whispered.

She turned from him and hurried down the street.

An old lady pulled at Ellen's sleeve. Ellen turned. Edward was walking away. The red of the roses gleamed like a puddle of blood in the road.

"Are the gates to the graveyard near here?"

"Where those flowers are," replied Ellen.

The old lady stared. "Them looks like roses."

"They are."

The old lady looked at Ellen's face and the bloodstained handkerchief she was clutching in her hands. "You lost someone, dearie?" she asked.

"My sister."

"That your young man?"

Ellen looked into the old lady's wizened face. She couldn't speak.

"The dead are in peace, my darling. It's the living that suffer." The old lady patted Ellen's hand as if she was a child. "Time will help. Good-bye, dear."

As Ellen walked down the street, her boots were heavy as lead and every bone in her body ached with misery.

Her life was falling apart and there was no comfort anywhere.

When Ellen opened the door, her parents' wagon stank like a pub. Norah was polishing a table with beer dregs. Ellen sat down and let the yeasty smell fill her nostrils. She was glad to see her mother doing something normal.

"Soup?"

"Yes, please."

Norah didn't ask where Ellen had been. They both knew she had been with Edward, but it didn't matter anymore. Ellen held the mug of hot soup in her hands.

Lucy's brand-new costume was hanging on the wall in front of her.

Norah rinsed out her beer-soaked cloth. Ellen sipped her soup.

The costume hung between them like a question.

"What will you do with it?" asked Ellen at last.

"That depends on you." Norah put down her piece of cloth. "I could let it out to fit you or I could pick it apart and sell it."

"My own costume will do," said Ellen uncertainly. Her head was spinning again. Why was she talking in riddles? Why was her mother doing the same? Hadn't either of them learned anything from Lucy's death?

Silence spread through the wagon.

They both looked at the glittering costume. The sleeves on the red satin jacket were edged with gold ruffles. It was fastened with gold toggles down the front. Ellen's costume had plain buttons. There were no ruffles on the sleeves.

"The gold braid would fetch something," said Ellen steadily.

Suddenly the despair she had felt at the cemetery turned to rage. The more she looked at the costume, the angrier she became. How dare Lucy die and leave everyone like this? It was selfish and unfair. All her life she'd made trouble. Now she was doing the same when she was dead.

"Don't be angry with her, Ellen."

Ellen looked away from the glittering costume. She knew that neither she nor her mother would truly recover from Lucy's death if they were still bound up in her lies.

"I have to talk to you." Ellen put down her cup of soup and told Norah everything. From her lessons with Alfred Montmorency to Lucy's engagement to Joe Morgan.

At the end of it, Norah buried her face in her hands and didn't move for a long time. Ellen sat watching her, not knowing whether to stay or leave her mother on her own.

"Don't leave," Norah mumbled. She reached out her hand

and Ellen took it. Her mother's hand was rough and wide like a man's. Now it was wet with tears. They sat in silence for a long time.

At last Norah looked up. Her face was still grey and haggard, but Ellen saw immediately that something had changed. There was a spark of light in her eyes.

"We have to start a new life, Ellen." Norah took a deep breath. "We have to let Lucy go." She shook her head and smiled sadly. "Such a one for telling lies, that girl. She'd have us all trussed up like a spider's dinner."

Norah squeezed Ellen's hand. "You've told me what you've told me. And I'm grateful to you. Let's leave it to settle, shall we?"

Ellen nodded.

They both looked across at Lucy's costume.

"Is there enough to let out?" Ellen asked.

Norah stood up and turned the costume inside out.

"I'd say so."

# EIGHT

ELLEN FINALLY MET JOE MORGAN WHEN SHE WENT WITH SAM to Newport's Animal Emporium. Sam had to buy a replacement rabbit for the one his ferret had eaten.

"Wotcha!" cried Sam.

Ellen looked around and saw a young man with straight black eyebrows and dark brown eyes. From Lucy's description of him and from what she had heard of him, she felt as if she knew something of Joe Morgan, even though they had never met. She also felt terribly guilty that she had never made the effort to seek him out after Lucy's death. But the idea that she might start rumours flying all over again had been too much to bear and now, looking into Joe's steady eyes, she thought he might understand.

The young man held out his hand to Ellen. "I'm Joe Morgan."

"I'm Ellen Spangle." Ellen took Joe's hand and shook it.

They held each other's gaze, and Ellen recognized something that connected them other than Lucy's death. Perhaps it was loyalty. At that moment, it occurred to Ellen that she might find a friend in Joe Morgan, or at least someone who would understand her feelings of loss at Lucy's death.

They stood clasped in a handshake that seemed to go on forever, both knowing they wanted to talk alone but with no idea how to go about it.

At last Ellen withdrew her hand and fiddled unnecessarily with the purse that hung from her belt.

"Don't worry about me," said Sam. "I'm off to buy a new ferret."

"But you've already got one," blurted Ellen. As soon as she said it, she realised how ridiculous she sounded.

Sam rolled his eyes. "If I get a new rabbit, my old ferret will only eat it."

Joe shot Ellen a sideways glance, seeing a way to be with her on his own. "Sam's quite right, as usual."

"Oh," said Ellen faintly.

Joe nodded and turned back to Sam. "Tell you what. Sid Barker's just got some fine young ferrets in. Tell him I sent you."

Sam grinned.

Sometimes he wondered if your brain got softer as you grew older. He knew perfectly well that Ellen and Joe wanted to be on their own.

He decided to make the most of it while he could. "Lend us a shilling, Ellen."

Ellen handed over the money without a murmur, as expected. Outside on the street, Sam turned and looked back through the window.

Ellen was standing with her head bowed as if she was listening intently. Joe stood opposite her, his arms making rapid jerky movements in the air.

"I've never been in a pub before." Ellen put her fingers around the sticky glass of fizzy lemonade. "Lucy always called this rattle belly pop." Ellen laughed nervously. She lifted the glass to her lips but put it down. Her hands were shaking too much. "I'm sorry, Joe. I should have come to find you after Lucy died." But even as she said it, they both knew why she hadn't.

Fred Spangle and Jeremiah Morgan.

"I should have looked for you," said Joe in a hoarse voice. "No one knows the truth except you." He rubbed his hands over his face. "I loved her so much, Ellen."

"I loved her too." Ellen realised that it was the first time she had said that to anyone. "Oh, Joe!" she cried suddenly. "I've been so unkind to you, and I'm so sorry. At least I have my family to comfort me, but you see it all happened so fast. It was as if my father wanted her under the ground before anyone had a chance to realise she was dead, and then everything—"

"Why did she have to be so *stupid*?" Joe almost shouted. "I told her again and again not to try a forward somersault. I knew no good would come of it."

"So did I." Ellen shrugged miserably. "But Lucy could never wait for anything."

"I don't know how I'll live without her."

"None of us do." Ellen dug her fingernails in her hand to

stop herself crying. "Sometimes I think my father is losing his mind."

Joe looked up and a darkness passed over his face. He remembered the last time he had seen Lucy. It was the afternoon before she died. She had sent him a message to meet her. He had never seen her so angry, so determined to prove to her father that he needed her more than she needed him. Joe was sure they must have had a terrible row. And it was then that he had promised to come and watch her. *You have to see me, Joe! You have to see how good I am! And then I'll tell you the best secret in the world!*

"Did something happen between Lucy and your father that day?"

Ellen decided she owed it to Joe to tell him everything that had taken place before Lucy died. Even so, there was so much she didn't know about his feelings for Lucy. Had Lucy loved him as much as he appeared to love her? Did he really believe he could trust Lucy? Indeed, was it true that they had come to an arrangement at all? Or had Lucy made that up to upset Ellen as much as she could? Looking into Joe's face, now Ellen found it almost impossible to believe that he would have encouraged her in such a rash plan. But then perhaps she was just seeing what she wanted to see. What did she really know of Joe Morgan?

Joe watched Ellen's face. "Tell me," he pleaded.

Ellen took a deep breath. Even if she did lose Joe's friendship, she made up her mind to tell him the truth. She couldn't live with any more lies.

"The night before she died we had a terrible quarrel." Tears filled Ellen's eyes and rolled down her cheeks. "I tried to make it up with her, but I didn't see her again until we went into the ring." Ellen shook her head. "Our lion was sick and my mother was too ill to look after it. So I had to." Ellen picked up her glass. But it was no good. She couldn't lift it to her mouth. "That afternoon Lucy and my father had a dreadful fight. I don't know what it was about, but she hit him with her whip and ran away." Ellen looked up. "I think that's when she made up her mind to try the somersault."

Joe was dumbfounded. "You didn't know?"

"No."

Joe stared at her with his mouth open. "She told me you knew. She met me that afternoon and told me she had to prove to her father how good she was because you wanted to leave the circus and that would leave her on her own." He put his head in his hands. "She told me I had to watch her that night because she had a secret to tell me."

Now it was Ellen who stared in utter disbelief. At the same moment, she felt her insides grow cold.

"The last time I saw Lucy she said you and she had come to an arrangement." In her mind's eye, Ellen saw Lucy's painted face twisted with fury. She heard her screaming, *I'm not propping you up any longer! I want a life of my own.*

Ellen gulped at her lemonade. Now she felt betrayed and furious. "Lucy said you were going to tell Father after the show!" Her hand had stopped shaking. "She meant me to understand she was going to leave home and join Morgan's as soon as you were married."

A strangled sound came from Joe's throat. "I loved her, Ellen, but we hadn't come to any arrangement." His face was filled with such hurt and misery Ellen could hardly bear to look at it. "Of course, we talked about a future." Joe shrugged hopelessly. "But she was only fourteen."

Ellen said nothing. Lucy had always twisted the truth to suit herself.

"I don't understand," muttered Joe. "Why did Lucy tell me she was trapped because of you?"

It occurred to Ellen that perhaps this was the first thing Lucy had said that could have been true. She leaned forward. "Maybe Lucy did feel trapped. The thing is, Joe, I've been taking lessons from a private tutor for two years now. I don't want to stay in the circus forever. I want to teach or be a governess."

"Lucy told me."

"What?"

"Outside the tea room," replied Joe. "She took me back there to make sure you were settled with Edward." Joe shook his head. "I guessed then that she was supposed be with you."

As he spoke, he remembered ignoring a definite feeling that he was being selfish and irresponsible falling in with Lucy's plans. But Lucy had been irresistible. He couldn't help himself. Joe groaned out loud.

Ellen didn't know what to think anymore. "I can't believe she told you about my lessons."

Joe frowned. "Why is that so important?"

"Because it was a secret between us," said Ellen. "We'd made a promise." She could see from Joe's face that he understood. "But you're right, she was supposed to be with me. That's what I agreed with my mother." Ellen felt her stomach turn over and over. "If only I'd had the courage to tell my mother the truth about my lessons, Lucy would never have been able to blackmail me."

Now Joe understood. "She called in the favour so she could meet me on her own," he said in a dead voice.

Ellen nodded.

"So if she had never walked out with me—"

"I didn't mean that!" cried Ellen.

But the more Ellen thought about it, the worse she felt. It was nothing to do with Joe. It was her own selfishness in wanting to see Edward that had allowed Lucy to become so involved with him. There was nothing Joe could have done to talk Lucy out of her craziness. She had lied to everyone around her.

Poor Joe felt as guilty as she did. They were both the kind of people who tried not to let others down. But what good had it done either of them? And was it so selfish of Ellen to want to be with the person she loved? As the thought of Edward went through her head, Ellen felt hollow. Something didn't feel right.

Ellen picked up her lemonade glass. Now her hand had started to shake again and she couldn't hold the glass. A few feet away, a barmaid heaved a huge steaming ham onto the bar and began to slice it. The sweet smell of the meat wafted over to their table.

"Are you hungry?"

"Yes," said Ellen.

Joe called out an order, and five minutes later two plate-fuls of ham and pickles with a hunk of crusty bread were put in front of them.

They ate quickly, in silence, but there was no uneasiness. For Ellen it was the first time she had felt comfortable with anyone for ages. But why did that make her feel guilty? The only thing between her and Joe Morgan was a shared memory of Lucy, even if that memory was difficult and painful. No, the guilt came from somewhere else. Ellen realised she needed someone she could trust absolutely, and there was something about Joe that filled that need. She couldn't let him go.

When he had finished, Joe pushed his plate away. "You can't leave your father's circus," he said quietly. "Not before you've trained someone to take your place. It wouldn't be fair."

Ellen found herself staring at a pudgy little man stuffing a mouthful of pink ham into his pink face. She had never thought of training a new person, and yet it was obvious. What's more, it let her believe there was a way to help her parents as well as planning a life for herself.

"And you can't leave Sam," said Joe flatly.

Ellen looked into Joe's steady, dark eyes. She knew he was right.

ஃ  ஃ  ஃ

Two weeks later Ellen told Edward that she had decided to stay with the circus for the summer tour. She didn't tell him she had discussed the subject with Joe Morgan. It didn't seem any of his business, and somehow she wanted to keep her friendship with Joe separate from her feelings for Edward. Especially since her friendship with Joe had deepened over the three occasions they had met in Greenwich since the chance encounter at Newport's Animal Emporium. It had been Sam's doing, and Ellen was sure no one had seen them together. Greenwich was a morning's walk from Fender's Field. It was just that talking to Joe about her mother and father and how she could carry on the act on her own had helped so much. Because Joe was part of the circus world and understood how it worked. In any case, Ellen knew Edward wouldn't object to her decision. He never questioned anything she said to him.

Now Edward stared at his lap. He didn't want to make the same mistake as he had with the roses, although he still didn't know what he'd done wrong. Of course the news that Ellen would be performing again was absolutely thrilling. But he understood that he had to choose his words carefully. He didn't want her to feel he was influencing her in any way.

"I trust you, dearest," he said at last. "You must do whatever you think best. I will wait for you forever."

Ellen took his hand and felt it tremble in her own. She looked into his face and saw sweat gleaming on his forehead. "Is something troubling you, Edward?"

Fear shot through Edward and a trickle of moisture ran down his neck. It would be too dreadful to mess things up now. What could he say?

He looked into Ellen's dark, serious eyes. "I love you."

Ellen waited on the edge of the ring. It was the first time she had performed without her sister since she was six. Then she had ridden on Fred's shoulders as he galloped around the ring. Ellen remembered it well. Every night Norah had dressed her in a glittering fairy costume, and every night Lucy had thrown a jealous tantrum. When they went to bed, Lucy had pinched her and pulled her hair.

Fred had never been able to understand why Ellen had been so quick to give up her place to her sister. The trumpets struck up. Ellen pushed the memory away. It was all over now.

"Ladies and gemmen," cried Fred. "Owing to the sad and tragic death of Seraphina Scarletta, the amazing Sapphire will perform on her own!" He turned and held out his arm. "Please welcome the incredible Sapphire Scarletta!"

Ellen cantered into the ring, standing up on Pearl's back. Fred hadn't seen her new costume, and she saw the surprise on his face.

She and Norah had agreed that Ellen's costume should be completely different. The scarlet satin jacket had changed to royal blue. Where there had been gold, now there was silver. Lucy's sequined skirt had become a frothy cloak edged with turquoise and silver. Instead of a feathery headdress, Ellen wore a single high comb of glittering paste.

She galloped around the ring. The frothy net cloak billowed out from her shoulders and made her look as if she was flying above Pearl's back. Now she didn't have to fit in with Lucy's showy gestures, and she rode with the grace and elegance that came naturally to her. At the precise moment when Pearl's stride was smoothest, Ellen held up her sparkling arms and twirled around backwards, then forwards. Then she slid down onto Pearl's haunches and lay full length along her back.

The crowd stood as one and roared. As Fred watched, he felt a steel band tighten around his chest. Ellen was a truly brilliant rider. Why had he never seen it before? Why did he still miss Lucy so much that sometimes he thought he would die from the sadness of it? Fred moved backwards into the shadows so his face was hidden. But no one noticed the ringmaster had gone. They were all staring at Ellen.

Ellen jumped lightly to her feet, bowed, then ran from the ring. The band played one encore and then another. Fred came to his senses and ran back into the ring.

"Ladies and gemmen! The one and only! The *sensational* Sapphire Scarletta!"

"Cor! Ellen! You was *miraculous*!" Jake was in his clown costume, ready for the next act. "I never knew you could ride like that!" He jerked his head backwards into the night. "Ludwig's so knocked back, 'e's gone to the tavern!"

Sam wrapped his arms around his sister's waist. "You were brilliant, Ellen. Everyone said so." As he spoke, he reached into his pocket and handed her a piece of crumpled paper.

Ellen opened it. *I knew you could do it! Joe.*

She stared at the paper. Then she jerked up her head.

"Was Joe here? Was he watching?"

Sam nodded, grinning. "All disguised he was. No one knew but me!"

Ellen almost burst out laughing. After each meeting with Joe, she felt easier about her memories of Lucy and more comfortable in herself. It was odd. Joe was the first person Ellen truly believed she could rely on. She felt she could talk to him about anything, although of course, they mostly talked about the circus. Maybe that kind of easiness was the sign of a good friendship. Maybe when you loved someone, it was all more difficult and painful—like with Edward. Ellen didn't ask herself any more questions. She just knew that she wanted to see Joe again.

Edward waited in an alleyway by the theatre. Around him the crowds broke up into groups and wandered into the streets. As soon as he was alone, Edward pulled a small knife from his pocket and slit around the edge of the new poster announcing Ellen's solo performance. *The Amazing Sapphire Scarletta.*

The blade was sharp and the job was neatly done. Edward rolled up his prize and walked quickly down the street.

# NINE

Spring arrived. Fender's Field gradually turned from a muddy wasteland into grassy patches speckled with daffodils and cow parsley. One day Sam grabbed Ellen's hand as she was setting out to sell her pots of liniment. He wore a bright new chequered wool shirt and corduroy trousers that Ellen had bought him the week before. She had more money now that she had put off her lessons with Alfred Montmorency until the following winter.

It had been difficult to tell him, and it would have been easier to write. But Alfred Montmorency had deserved to be told face-to-face. Besides, he had lent her his copy of Keats's poems, and now that she had Edward's present she felt it was only fair to return Alfred's to him.

Alfred Montmorency had been surprised when the parlour maid announced that a Miss Pearl Rowley was waiting in the hall. When she had come to pay her debts a while ago, she had not mentioned another lesson in the immediate future. Not wishing to embarrass her in case she was having financial difficulties, Alfred had suggested books she could borrow from the library and wished her good luck.

Now Pearl Rowley stood in front of him. He was struck, as he always was, by the stillness and strength of her presence.

"Do sit down, Miss Rowley," said Alfred. He shifted a pile of paper from the only other chair in the room. "I'm sorry, I wasn't expecting visitors."

"Please," said Ellen. "I don't want to disturb you."

At the sound of her voice, Jasper ran from his cushion in the corner of the room and scrabbled at her skirts.

"Jasper!" cried Alfred.

Ellen picked the terrier up and Jasper lay his head in her lap as if he wanted to stay there forever.

"He's had no recurrence of the pain," said Alfred awkwardly. He could tell that Miss Rowley had something difficult to say. He was sure he knew what it was. "I'm very grateful to you."

"Not at all. I am glad I could help him."

Ellen reached into her purse and put Alfred's tattered book of poems on the table in such a way that confirmed his suspicions.

He picked up the book. It fell open at "Ode to a Nightingale." "It would seem we both like this poem."

"It is my favourite one." Now that she was here, Ellen felt she owed Alfred Montmorency some kind of explanation for her decision. After all, she had been coming to him for two years. But what could she say? She had no idea when she would return to him.

"I have enjoyed our lessons, Miss Rowley," said Alfred,

seeing the look of confusion on Ellen's face. "Not many of my pupils are of your calibre."

Ellen smiled ruefully. "So you have guessed why I am here."

Alfred felt strangely depressed. This young woman had such a fine mind. It would be a terrible shame if she abandoned her studies. He thought of his own circumstances. "Please excuse me, but if it is a question of finances—"

Pearl Rowley shook her head. Her eyes were dark and fathomless and there was a heightened curve to her cheekbones. Alfred was sure something drastic had happened to her.

"That is kind of you," said Ellen. "It isn't a financial decision. My sister died. I have decided to stay with my family for the time being." She smiled at him. "I am very grateful for your concern. My lessons with you have"—she paused to choose her words carefully—"changed my life."

Alfred felt the colour rise in his cheeks. He stared down at the book of poems. Suddenly he wanted to give her something, if only to remind her of him. "Would you accept this book from me?" He dipped his pen into an inkwell. "I would like to think it might give you some enjoyment during your difficult times."

"Thank you," said Ellen. How odd it was that she should now own two copies of the same precious book. How strange her life had become.

They stood up. Alfred handed her the book of poems. "It was given to me at a time when my own studies were interrupted."

As Ellen put the book in her purse, the last line of "Ode to a Nightingale" flashed through her mind.

*Fled is that music:—Do I wake or sleep?*

"Ellen!" cried Sam. "Yes or no?"

"Sorry, Sam," said Ellen vaguely. "Yes or no, what? I was thinking about something else."

Sam stared at his sister. She was strange these days. Sometimes she was happy, and the next moment she was sad. Sam didn't understand. "Can you come with me for half an hour?"

"Where?"

"To get some fireworks."

"What for?"

"Don't you know *anything*?"

"More than you if your reading and writing is anything to go by," said Ellen. "Anyway, what do you need fireworks for?"

Sam's eyes gleamed. "I've saved up some money with—" He clamped his hand over his mouth.

"You don't have to keep secrets from me," said Ellen, pinching his ear. "I know you're showing your Happy Families Cage with Joe Morgan."

Sam's eyes widened. "Pa hasn't found out, has he?"

"Of course not," replied Ellen. "You'd hear about it if he had."

While everyone in the circus was coming to terms with

Lucy's death, Fred seemed unable to shake off his despair. Night after night, Norah said, he groaned and muttered beside her. In the mornings his face was so dark, his family had learned to avoid him. Nothing was right and everything seemed to irritate him. Ellen's growing reputation as a solo performer only seemed to make things worse.

Ellen knew that Sam spent more and more time with Joe, and even though she knew it was ridiculous, she found herself feeling almost jealous of him.

Sam chattered beside her. "Joe's got a Siamese cat, three canaries, and a big black rat." He laughed. "Joe says the rat reminds him of his father."

Ellen thought of the last time she had talked to Joe. After they had discussed problems with horses, they had returned to the subject of Lucy. Joe had said then that he was almost positive Jeremiah knew nothing of his relationship with Lucy. As for Fred, Ellen was sure he had heard no more than drunken whispering, otherwise Lucy would have been under lock and key in an animal cage.

"It's strange," Joe had said. "The more I think about it, the more I see that Lucy and my father were alike."

At first Ellen hadn't been able to see what he was talking about. Then suddenly she had understood. Jeremiah was ruthless but he had the charisma of a pirate. He twisted people around his little finger and always he got what he wanted.

Just like Lucy had done.

Then Joe had stared at her. "But how could I have loved one and still hate the other?"

That had been at least two weeks ago, and she had heard nothing from him since then.

"Ellen!" cried Sam, pulling at his sister's arm. "You aren't listening again! I said Joe is getting a buzzard!"

"Sorry, Sam."

They had come to the end of a narrow street, which opened onto a square. Mrs. Hallward's Tea Room was on the corner. "What on Earth are we doing here?"

Sam followed Ellen's gaze. "What's so special about a stuffy old tea shop?"

"Nothing."

"Yes, there is," insisted Sam. "Your face has gone pink."

"If you must know, it's where I met Edward," said Ellen. But now she felt guilty because she had been thinking of Joe. Although she told herself time and time again that there was no reason to feel guilty. Joe was only a friend. And you could miss someone you liked as much as someone you loved.

"Oh," said Sam in a dull voice. He didn't like Edward much but knew better than to say so. Edward had given him a new hoop and stick. But it was so posh, Sam was embarrassed by it. As a result, he never showed it to his friends and couldn't join in when they played hoops together.

Suddenly Ellen was cross. "I said, what are we doing here?"

Sam stared at his sister. "Why are you angry with me?"

"I'm not angry. I asked you a question. Twice."

But Ellen knew she *was* angry. She was angry at herself for not being able to understand what she really felt for Edward. Was it love? Edward hadn't visited her for over a month now, and while she missed him, she also felt a certain relief at not having to explain herself to him.

Little by little, everyone in the circus was getting used to Lucy's death, but each person had his or her own way of coping. It seemed to Ellen that she had hidden inside herself, and only someone who had known Lucy as she really had been could help her. And that person was Joe. Every day Ellen felt stronger. Soon she hoped to be able to move back into the world again, with Edward at her side.

"*You* have to buy them," Sam was saying. He pointed to a fireworks shop. "The old man won't sell them to me."

Ellen wasn't looking. "Buy what?"

"Fireworks, for gawd's sake!" cried Sam. "I told you already!"

"Don't you swear at me!" snapped Ellen. "What do you need fireworks for?"

Sam took a deep breath and fought to get his own temper back. It would be silly to come all this way for nothing. Besides, he had promised Joe. "You know Mr. Foley that owns the Bunch of Grapes Tavern?" He tried to speak calmly, although he felt like shouting. "Well, him being Irish and it being St. Patrick's Day, he's putting on a big fireworks party next to Fender's Field." He paused. "You can only join in if you bring a firework."

"That's ridiculous," snapped Ellen. "St. Patrick's Day was two weeks ago! Besides, you don't have to *bring* one. You can just look over the field."

"What does it matter when St. Patrick's Day was!" shouted Sam, almost in tears. "If everyone did that, there wouldn't be hardly any fireworks."

He grubbed around in his pockets and handed her two dirty half crowns. "Joe asked me to get him a couple of rockets. I've saved some money too."

"Joe?" cried Ellen. "What's Joe got to do with this?"

"I promised Joe I'd get some for him," wailed Sam. "Why are you so cross? It's just a party. Joe said everyone was wanting a good night."

Ellen could hear Joe saying it. Her mood lifted. "Is he coming?"

Sam nodded. *"Everyone's* coming, Ellen! I told you!"

A bell tinkled as Ellen pushed opened the door. Inside, the shop stank of rotten eggs.

Sam wrinkled his nose. "What's that smell?"

"Sulphur," said Ellen. "They use it to make fireworks."

An old man shuffled towards them. He had a face like a smoked kipper. "What can I do for you, miss?"

"We would like to buy some fireworks, please," said Ellen.

"Rockets? Fizzers? Bangers?" The old man pointed around him. The walls were lined from floor to ceiling with shelves stacked with different-size boxes. Some were wrapped in brown paper and others in bright red tissue.

Ellen put her hand in her purse and felt for two half crowns. If Joe was putting up that much, it seemed only fair to match it.

"How many rockets can I buy for five bob?"

Sam gasped but said nothing. He was terrified she might change her mind. He dumped a pile of pennies, thruppenny bits, and sixpence beside the large silver coins on the counter. "Three and eleven. Add mine to 'ers."

"Happy occasion, is it?"

"Yes," said Ellen and Sam together, and laughed.

The shopkeeper piled up the money on the counter. "Got another bob for something special?"

Ellen opened her purse.

The man climbed up a ladder and took down an enormous rocket. "Left over from Guy Fawkes," he said. "Made it meself."

"So," said Ludwig, at Ellen's side. "This is what they mean by ze luck of ze Irish."

They stared at a bonfire the size of a small pyramid in the next-door field. All day men and children had dragged broken furniture and bits of timber from the riverbank—even the skeleton of a rowing boat—and stacked it all into a pile.

Now Ellen stood with Ludwig, watching sparks and flames shoot into the sky. Mr. Foley had indeed been lucky. It was the first dry night in two weeks. In the light from the flames, Ellen could see people clustered in groups, laughing and talking. Joe had been right. Everyone was ready for a party.

In one corner of the field, the Spangle hands had spread out an old piece of canvas. Families sat around a pile of potatoes and greasy pigs' trotters. Jugs of beer were lined up on the grass. Ellen could see her mother talking and laughing and it made her glad.

There was no sign of her father.

Beside her, Ludwig took a long gulp from a pewter mug. A steamy smell of rum and hot water wafted into the air. "I must talk to you about your father," he said.

"I'm going back to look for him after the fireworks," replied Ellen.

Ludwig shook his head. "That's my job. I said I would stay with the animals tonight, but he refused."

Ellen looked sideways at Ludwig's pewter mug and wondered if that was the reason her father had insisted on looking after the animals on his own.

"I know what you are thinking and you are wrong." Ludwig held up his mug. "So you had to care for Claudius. I had to care for your father. Yes, sometimes I drink too much, but not since that night." He stared at Ellen. "Your father is in a terrible despair."

Ellen turned away. "Why are you telling me something I know? I've spoken to my mother. What we can do?"

"You are not understanding me," said Ludwig, almost angrily. "Your father is losing his wits."

The sky exploded with noise and stinking smoke. A thousand jewel-coloured sparks fluttered down to the ground.

Ellen looked up and cried out, like everyone else in the field. When she turned back, Ludwig was gone and Sam was there standing beside a stockily built young man whose face was blacked out with soot and whose eyes had bright blue circles painted under them.

Ellen felt her heart surge in her chest. "Joe," she whispered.

Joe stared at Ellen's long, beautiful face and felt the same tenderness as he had felt when they last met. It seemed then and it seemed now that his friendship with Ellen was becoming more and more important in his life. Without her, he would never have been able to come to terms with losing Lucy, and he hoped that he had been able to help her as much as she had helped him.

Before Joe could speak to Ellen, Sam jabbed him in the ribs. "It's our rocket next! They kept it for last!"

There was a deafening blast. They both looked up. Red and gold sparks glittered in the sky like sequins.

"Cor!" cried Sam.

Ellen went rigid.

"Jesus Christ," muttered Joe. Instinctively, he reached out and took Ellen's hand.

It was as if Lucy was looking down at them.

# TEN

Fred Spangle tossed and turned in a nightmare. A choking smell pricked his nose and made his eyes itchy. With a sickening sense of dread, he woke up. The wagon was full of smoke. He turned and shook Norah as hard as he could. "Get up! Get up! We're on fire!" He pulled on his boots and trousers and yanked open the wagon door.

A great column of greasy black smoke was pouring out of the little shed beside the stables. It was where the tallow pots and rags were kept for the circus torches. Fred fought back the urge to scream. A spark from the fireworks must have somehow landed on a rag. Suddenly the shed exploded and a fireball burst upwards and sideways. Flames snaked along the roof towards the stables.

"Fetch the water men!" yelled Fred to Norah. "I'll see to the animals!"

He ran into the field. All around him men and women were throwing props out of sheds and carrying them away from the fire. The crackling of the flames was deafening. "Never mind the bloody props!" screamed Fred. "Move your wagons!"

At the far end of the field, but still not far enough to be

safe if the fire spread, Ludwig and Jake were harnessing the wagon that carried the animal cages to two cart horses. It was a dangerous job. Claudius was leaping back and forth and banging against the wooden walls at either end of his cage. Beside him the hyenas threw themselves at the bars, desperately trying to escape. At any minute, the cage could topple over and smash on the ground.

"Get them out of here!" bellowed Fred.

Ludwig did up the last heavy strap on the cart horses' harness. "Pull!" he shouted. He grabbed the horses' halters and dragged them forwards. But the smoke in the air frightened the huge animals, and it took all of Ludwig's skill to stop them from lunging out of control.

A gusty breeze blew bits of burning planks about like matchsticks. Norah ran back into the field. Ellen and Sam were hurriedly throwing what belongings they could lift through the door of the family wagon. The roof was burning. It wouldn't be long before the whole wagon was on fire.

"Where's Father?" screamed Ellen. "The stables are burning!"

A handbell jangled in the night. The fire cart rattled down the street and stopped in the field. Three men jumped down and began to pull a long canvas hose across the grass. It was slow, heavy work. Ellen watched in agony as the hose came nearer and nearer to the stables.

"Man the pump!" cried a water man. He raised his arm to signal to the men waiting by the fire cart. They began pumping as hard as they could. Everyone waited for the water to gush out of the hose and douse the flames.

A trickle dribbled onto the ground.

"Where's the water?" shouted Fred. Above the sound of the fire, he could hear his horses squealing with terror.

"The pump's broken, mate," gasped the water man. "Gawd help you."

"Gawd help my 'osses, you bastard!" Fred ran over to where the workers were standing by their wagons. "Make a chain! We'll use buckets!"

Five minutes later a human chain passed buckets of water hand to hand and threw them at the burning stables. Nothing stopped the flames. The water only seemed to spread them further.

By now smoke was pouring out of the stable roof. The horses screamed and whinnied. They beat their hooves against the walls, desperately trying to break their way out.

"Keep 'em coming!" yelled Fred. "It's our only chance."

Bucket after bucket was thrown at the burning building. But it was too late. The walls were on fire. The roof was about to fall in.

Suddenly Fred picked up a bucket of water and tipped it over his head. Then, before anyone realised what he was up to, he ran through the door into the burning stables.

"Stop him!" screamed Norah. "He's gone mad!" She ran after him, but Jake grabbed her by the shoulders. "Keep up the chain!" bellowed Ludwig. "Give him a chance!"

Buckets passed from hand to hand, faster than ever. Norah stood as if made out of stone.

Ellen ran over to Jake. "Fill a barrel with water and soak a blanket!" she shouted. "When my father comes out, drench him and wrap him in the blanket!"

Jake looked at her as if she was crazy.

"Do it!" yelled Ellen, furious that Jake didn't understand. "If he comes out, he'll be on fire."

A shower of sparks burst into the night. The far end of the stables had collapsed. The buckets stopped moving. No one could do anything but stare at the door. The first smell of burning horsehair floated into the night. Suddenly the horses galloped out of the door. They went in every direction, squealing and whinnying with terror.

"Stand back!" yelled Ludwig. "Give them room!" He knew that if the horses saw their way blocked, they could panic and run back into the flames. The men stumbled backwards and cleared a path as fast as they could.

Ellen counted the horses as they thundered across the field. Some clattered into the streets. But that didn't matter. They were all there. They'd come back tomorrow.

The wooden frame of the door crashed into flames and fell sideways. Fred Spangle stumbled out from underneath it. His entire body was on fire.

"Jake!" screamed Ellen.

But Jake was already there with Ludwig. They tipped up

the barrel and drenched the burning thing that collapsed on the ground. Then they covered him in the sodden blanket.

Edward de Lacy sat in the dark breakfast room of his parents' house in Notting Hill Gate. The maid took away his bowl of porridge and put a plate of sausages and eggs in front of him.

His mother and father sat at either end of the table. As usual, no one spoke. Lady Amelia always read the *Illustrated London News* at breakfast. Sir Winston stayed firmly behind a copy of the *Times* that had been specially ironed for him.

He leaned to the left. The parlour maid moved quickly from the sideboard and refilled his cup of tea from a silver pot. It was Sir Winston's habit to drink three cups of strong tea before he rose from the table and attended to his morning appointments. This morning Sir Winston was out of sorts. He stabbed angrily at his food and rattled the pages of his newspaper.

Edward ate his breakfast as quickly and quietly as possible. He knew why his father was in a bad mood.

The day before, Sir Winston had unexpectedly visited Edward in his studio. The exhibition Lady Amelia was organising had been arranged for Easter, and Sir Winston wanted to see for himself what his son had been doing with his time. When he walked into the room, the walls were bare. There were no canvases stacked on the floor. There was only a table drawer bulging with half-finished sketches.

"Where are your paintings?" Sir Winston had demanded.

Six months before, he had agreed with his wife that Edward should be allowed the chance to learn to paint. After that, if he showed no talent, he would go to medical school.

"I would prefer not to show them to you until they are finished," replied Edward uneasily. He pretended to tidy his brushes so he wouldn't have to look at his father's face.

Although the two men looked similar, Sir Winston knew his son was much more like his wife. Lady Amelia lived in a fantasy world. At the moment, she was playing the role of a salon hostess for the artists and writers among her friends. Edward's upcoming exhibition filled every moment of her day. *Of course my son is a painter.*

Sir Winston tried not to show the fury that was boiling inside him. For weeks he had watched Edward moon about as if he was in a continuous daydream. He was hardly ever at home, but now it was clear he hadn't been spending much time in his studio, either.

"Surely the portrait of your mother must be finished."

"I've sent it to be framed," lied Edward. "Mother said a good frame creates a good impression."

Sir Winston cleared his throat. Certainly his wife knew a lot about creating good impressions. It was the foundation on which she had built her life. "Quite," he muttered. He put on his top hat and opened the door. "I wish you a profitable day."

Now Sir Winston stood up from the breakfast table and accidentally knocked over his chair. It hit the floor with a startling crash in the silent room. Lady Amelia detested unexpected events. She jumped, and her porcelain cup jerked in her hand. Tea slopped all over the white linen tablecloth. The parlour maid ran from her place by the sideboard and mopped up the mess. Sir Winston picked up his chair and walked over to his wife. As he passed, Edward could sense his father was about to say something to him. He put a sausage in his mouth so he would have an excuse not to answer.

As Sir Winston bent down to kiss his wife's cheek, the newspaper slipped from his hand and fell open on the floor.

Edward looked down. The headline was short and the article small: FIRE AT FENDER'S FIELD. SPANGLE'S CIRCUS DAMAGED. Edward inhaled a mouthful of sausage and spluttered. He grabbed a napkin and held it to his mouth.

Lady Amelia looked up, startled. "Darling! Are you choking?"

"Of course he's not choking," snapped Sir Winston. "But his manners belong in the nursery."

"Really, Winston," replied Lady Amelia. "You are quite out of sorts this morning."

Edward mumbled his excuses and ran out of the dining room. As he opened the front door, he heard his father's booming voice. "Amelia! That boy needs to be taken in hand. I visited—"

Edward closed the front door and ran down the steps. All he could think of was Ellen. He cursed his mother's sister, who had been visiting with her family from Cumbria. She had stayed on an extra week and his mother had insisted that Edward show his nephews around London. He hadn't been able to get out to see Ellen for more than a month, and sending a message to Fender's Field was so unreliable.

"You've been away so much recently, darling," Lady Amelia had murmured. "The least you can do is help me out now."

Once Edward had suggested taking his nephews to the circus. At least then he would be able to see Ellen. "All the way to Whitechapel!" protested Lady Amelia. She shuddered. "Certainly *not*!"

The one day Edward had managed to escape to his studio, his father had appeared. By the time Sir Winston left, Edward's chance to visit Ellen was gone. It was all *too* unfair.

Edward pulled open the front gates.

There was no sign of an omnibus. He turned and saw a hansom cab standing on the corner. He ran up to it and asked the driver to take him to Whitechapel.

The driver stared at the dishevelled young man, still clutching a breakfast napkin in his hand. "Question is, can we afford it, sir?" he said, not moving from his seat to open the door.

Edward threw a sovereign into the cabbie's lap and yanked open the door. "I'm in a hurry!"

It seemed at first that Fred Spangle hadn't suffered the deep burns that Ellen and Norah feared. Jake and Ludwig had carried his smouldering body, wrapped in the wet blanket, to Ludwig's wagon. They had stripped off his clothes and wrapped him in a cotton bedspread. Ellen dosed him with opium and they waited.

Now Ellen looked down at her father's sleeping face. His skin had a glossiness to it. He looked healthy and rosy, as if he had been hop picking in Kent.

Two days later, on the morning Edward read the article in the newspaper, the skin on Fred's body fell off in strips. By the end of the day, he was covered in patches of raw oozing flesh.

Ellen sat in a chair beside her father's bed. She was half-asleep but aware of her father breathing beside her. Suddenly he jerked up in bed. His arms flailed at his sides and saliva frothed around his mouth. Then his body went rigid and his eyes rolled back in his head. Ellen caught him before he fell onto the floor. She wedged him against the wall with a rolled-up blanket and ran screaming from the wagon.

She bumped straight into Edward.

"Ellen! My dearest! Thank God, you're unhurt!" He put his hands on either side of her arms.

"Father's had a fit!" she cried. She shook away from his hold. "I'm sorry, Edward. I have to find my mother!" She was about to run on when Edward took hold of her arm and pulled her back.

"I'll ask my father to come."

Ellen stopped. "Would he really come out here? If anyone could save Pa, your father could!" She looked into Edward's worried, wide-eyed face. "Oh, Edward! I'd be grateful forever!"

In his mind's eye, Edward saw his father in his top hat and tailcoat step down from his carriage. He saw him hurry across the field. The circus people stared in amazement.

Some of the women curtseyed nervously as he passed. And afterwards, when he had treated Fred Spangle, Edward would introduce him to Ellen, and Sir Winston would recognise her goodness and worth immediately.

Edward looked down at the face that he worshipped. "Of course he'll come. Tell your mother to wait. I'll fetch him immediately."

"Will he be long?" asked Ellen urgently. "Pa is so very ill."

"He'll be here as soon as he can." Edward took her hand again. "I promise."

Ellen grabbed his hands and pulled them towards her. "Thank you. Thank you," she whispered.

Edward held her for as long as he dared. Then he turned and ran.

Ellen watched as Edward disappeared into the busy street. Tears of relief poured down her cheeks. But even as she stood in the muddy field, she knew she hadn't missed him.

She pushed the thought from her mind. It was too distressing. She owed her father's life to Edward's kindness.

"Got a penny, mister?" A ragged girl plucked at Edward's coat.

Edward ignored her and walked quickly down the street. A dray trundled past with two wooden barrels tied to the boards. Three boys rode on the back with their legs dangling above the muddy street. The wheels churned through a puddle and splashed Edward with dirty brown water. The boys pointed and laughed.

"A farthing'd do!" begged the girl. She tugged Edward's coat again.

Edward looked down at her grimy face. She smiled. All her teeth were black. He put out his hand and pushed her away. "Leave me alone, you filthy guttersnipe!"

Alfred Montmorency was in a print shop on Ravens Lane when he saw Edward de Lacy hurrying past the window. He quickly paid for a quire of foolscap paper and two new pen nibs and ran after him.

"Edward!"

Edward turned and gaped. "Alfred! How are you?"

"I'm well." Alfred stared at Edward's pale, sweating face. "Is something wrong?"

"No, no!" Edward's hands jumped at his side. "I'm going home to get my father." He jerked his head backwards. "You heard of the fire?"

"At that circus?" asked Alfred in a puzzled voice.

"Yes, yes. You see, Mr. Spangle is badly burned. They say he's had a seizure." Edward pulled a handkerchief from his pocket and rubbed it over his face. "I promised I would fetch Father to treat him."

Alfred stared at his friend as if he had gone crazy. "Edward! What on Earth are you saying? Your father would never treat a showman!"

Edward frowned. There was something in Alfred's voice that sounded absolutely certain, and it worried him.

He began to feel confused about what he had done.

"Out the way, mister! Out the way!" Edward stared stupidly as angry people walked past him. He had no idea he was blocking the way.

Alfred took Edward by the arm. He wondered whether his friend had suffered some kind of nervous collapse. What was he doing out here, anyway? "Edward," he said gently. "Your father would be appalled if he knew what you have done. You must never tell him."

Alfred knew that Sir Winston would be more than appalled, he would be seriously worried. Once again he wondered whether Edward was ill.

Edward looked around him at the grimy, weasel-eyed faces in the crowded street. It was all so *squalid*. All the pictures he had made up of Fender's Field and his father's visit began to fade. He started to feel more and more confused. Sweat poured out of him. Alfred was such a steady chap, even if he was a bore. Edward began to wonder whether he should explain to him how he had come to know the circus so well. Then Ellen's face floated in front of him, and Edward remembered she had been Alfred's pupil. Alfred would be furious with him. Then again, Alfred was on the spot.

"What shall I do?" asked Edward. His voice sounded peevish. "I gave my word."

"Circus people look after their own," said Alfred in a soothing voice. "Why on Earth would they ask a stranger? You must have misunderstood them."

Alfred clapped his arm around his friend's shoulder. "You really are much too softhearted," he said firmly. "Believe me, these people don't want the likes of you and me poking about in their lives. We don't understand them and they don't understand us."

Edward felt himself being taken to a place that was easy and familiar. "Perhaps you're right."

"Of course I'm right!" Alfred took Edward's arm. "I'd say you could do with some medicine yourself. How about a mug of the best bitter at the Sheaf of Barley?"

Edward nodded. Alfred was right. Ellen's family would only resent him if he tried to take over their lives. It was best to let them handle things in their own way. The last thing he wanted to do was make things more difficult for Ellen.

Edward allowed himself to be led down the street.

# ELEVEN

"Edward's father will come, Mother," said Ellen. "Edward promised."

Norah shook her head. Outside, dusk was falling. They had waited for most of the day. Beside her, Fred lay on a wooden pallet in the middle of the wagon. He was breathing rapidly and his burns were raw and weeping. The whites of his eyes looked horribly bright against the red and peeling mess that was his face. He hadn't spoken since his fit that morning.

Footsteps sounded on the steps up to the door.

"That's him!" cried Ellen. Despite herself, she pushed back the tendrils of hair that had fallen out of her bun and smoothed her skirt.

Norah, too, was nervous. She stepped back into a corner. "You open it. You talk to him. You explain."

Ellen put her hand on the doorknob. Should she curtsey? She was sure he knew nothing about her and Edward. They had agreed to keep their understanding quiet—at least until Edward inherited his aunt's estate.

The door opened and Joe Morgan stood in front of her.

"Joe!" cried Ellen. She was so surprised to see him, she almost stumbled. They stared at each other and Ellen found herself unable to speak. The relief she felt at seeing him was like a pain in her chest, and yet she was overwhelmed with disappointment that it wasn't Edward's father standing on the steps. She shook her head and forced herself to speak. "Joe. I'm sorry, I thought—," but she couldn't finish her sentence, and for a moment she thought she would burst into tears.

"Ellen," said Joe gently. He seemed to steady her with his eyes. "I came to help if I can."

Ellen pushed back the hair that had fallen out of her bun and leaned against a heavy table. "We're waiting for Edward's father," she said in a halting voice. "Sir Winston de Lacy is one of the best doctors in London." Ellen felt her voice stick in her throat. "He can save Father. I'm sure of it."

Joe looked at Norah, who was hunched in a chair. Her eyes were dull and staring. "How long have you been waiting?"

"All day," said Norah in a hollow voice.

"He'll come!" cried Ellen, half turning towards her mother. "He promised."

"Who promised?" asked Joe.

"Edward did."

As Ellen spoke, Joe saw the first flicker of uncertainty pass over her face. Then he watched her try to hide the hurt and pain that came with it, helpless to comfort her and dumb-founded that she would ever believe such a promise.

Joe's heart ached for her, but he knew they had to act quickly if there was to be a chance to save Fred. He chose his words carefully but spoke in a firm voice. "Ellen," said Joe. "A man like Sir Winston de Lacy would never come here. Surely you understand that." He knew that what he was saying was like pushing a knife into Ellen's body and then twisting it, but there was nothing else he could do.

Ellen sat down and buried her face in her hands. The niggling doubt she had hidden in the back of her mind exploded into a terrible stomach-churning conviction. Joe was right. Edward's father wasn't going to come. How could she ever have been stupid enough to think that he would? Now they had lost a whole day waiting. She dug her nails into her palm to stop herself from howling.

Joe looked at Fred's raw, rigid body. "How long has he been like this?"

"He had a fit this morning," said Ellen. Her voice was barely more than a croak.

"You must call a doctor," cried Joe.

"What doctor?" shouted Ellen, suddenly furious. She looked into Joe's grey face. "I'm sorry, Joe. I'm not angry with you. It's me."

Joe fought a huge urge to wrap Ellen in his arms and comfort her. He had learned a lot from Sam and realised now that Ellen was the rock in her family. She had looked after Lucy. She had looked after Sam. Now she was trying to save her father.

Joe watched Ellen's shoulders drooping. He knew her world was falling apart and she was losing her strength. But still he didn't go near her. For her own sake as much as his. If she collapsed now, she would be no help to her father.

"I know a doctor," muttered Norah. She stood up and wrapped a shawl around her shoulders. "Please God, he's not in the pub." She stepped into the murky evening light.

At first Moses Abernethy had refused to get up from his table. The tavern fire burned brightly and his whisky shone like amber in his glass. He was discussing his philosophy of life with amiable companions. Then the woman had offered him two sovereigns and he'd changed his mind.

Now he looked down at the red peeling thing that had once been a man. Surgeon Abernethy had seen burns like these from gas explosions in the mines when he worked in Yorkshire. Even the men who made it up to the surface were usually dead the next day.

He felt the sovereigns in his waistcoat pocket. Moses Abernethy went through the motions he'd been paid for. He felt for Fred's pulse and peered into his face. The man's breath was foul and his breathing rapid. It was unlikely he'd survive the night.

"These are deep burns," said Moses Abernethy solemnly. "A poultice of vinegar must be applied twice daily. The body must be bathed in oil of turpentine and the patient given a mild stimulant." He took out a notebook, scribbled on a page, and put the page on the table.

He turned to the woman in the shawl. It was customary to offer a visiting doctor some refreshment. Surgeon Abernethy cleared his throat. Surely even circus people must be aware of such basic courtesies.

"Have you wine at hand?" he asked Ellen at last. Surgeon Abernethy was thirsty. He was damned if he was going to go back through the night with a cold stomach.

Ellen shook her head. She couldn't speak for the fury that surged through her. The wagon stank of the surgeon's whisky breath. She knew what her mother had paid him and that what he had prescribed would kill her father through pain and shock. Let alone the fact that the burns were likely to turn septic.

"Sherry?" Surgeon Abernethy tried to keep the irritation out of his voice.

Norah put a bottle of brandy on the table but didn't open it.

No one spoke.

As the surgeon's hand reached towards the bottle, Ellen's anger exploded.

"You're a quack and you're drunk!" She picked up the bottle of brandy and banged it back on the shelf. "I wouldn't treat a dog like that!"

Surgeon Abernethy's face went white. The cramped, dark wagon reminded him of a sheep pen. It stank like one too. "Then perhaps you should treat your father yourself," he sneered. "I'm sure a circus girl who knows better than a surgeon must be able to work miracles."

He let the last word hang in the air.

Joe stepped forward. "Are you saying he will die?"

Surgeon Abernethy picked up his bag. "He'll be dead by the morning." He walked out of the wagon without closing the door.

Norah began to sob quietly.

Joe shut the door. "The quack's right, Ellen."

"That my father's going to die?"

"No. That you should treat him yourself."

Ellen shook her head hopelessly. "What do I know?"

"You know about sick animals." Joe touched her hand. "Ellen, that's all your father is now."

"But what if he dies?"

"Claudius lived."

"He's not a stinking old lion!" cried Ellen.

Fred groaned and sought out Ellen's face with his eyes.

"Ellen," said Joe in a low voice. "For God's sake, he's asking you to help him."

Ellen turned to her mother.

"I don't have your touch, lass." Norah looked at Fred. "He knows that."

Ellen bent down and put her lips to her father's ear. "God help me, Father," she whispered. "I'll try."

Two hours later the wagon was bare and scrubbed clean. With Norah's help Ellen smoothed an ointment of oil, pure white wax, and powdered lavender over her father's burns. She prayed that the lavender would be enough to stop the burns from going bad. They lit a candle and sat by his bed and waited.

Dawn was streaked with red and orange and the clouds that were piled up in the sky were edged with gold. Ellen looked across to where her mother was slumped in her chair. Beside her, Fred lay like a corpse wrapped in his white sheet. In the half light, it was impossible to tell if he was breathing or not. Ellen sat for a moment and looked at her father. He seemed to have shrunk. People always looked smaller when they were dead. Hadn't Lucy looked like a doll? Ellen felt as if she was made out of stone. She tried to get up, but she couldn't move.

Through the window beyond where her father lay, the sky grew brighter and the sun rose. A beam of light passed through the window and fell across the top half of Fred's body. His red hair was suddenly bright like a halo. Ellen felt a scream rising in her throat. The idea that in a second she would touch her father's arm and find it had turned cold was too terrible to bear. She reached out her hand.

The skin was warm. Fred was alive.

Ellen quietly opened the door and stepped down out of the wagon. She rushed across the field and over the street to her lodgings. Sam was curled up in her bed, fast asleep. Ellen shook him awake.

"Pa's alive, Sam! Pa's alive! The quack said he wouldn't live through the night!"

Sam jumped up in bed and threw his arms around his sister's neck. "You saved him, Ellen," he cried. "Joe said you would."

"It's only the beginning, Sam." Ellen tried to make her voice sound strong. "And we've got a long way to go but—" She burst into tears. If it hadn't been for Joe, she would never have had the courage to try. She wished more than anything that she could thank him face-to-face.

Ellen squeezed her brother hard against her. "Tell Joe," she said in a cracked voice, "tell him we did the right thing. I'd go myself but I can't leave Pa."

Sam clung to his sister. "Joe'll understand," he whispered. "And he'll be back. I know he will."

For the next two weeks, neither Norah nor Ellen left Fred's side. Every day they changed his dressings and gave him a cordial of opium and treacle. It was the only way to keep him still. As the days passed and her father began to get steadily better, Ellen was constantly reminded of Claudius and what Joe had said that night.

If only she could speak to him herself. Sam had said Joe would come to see her, but he hadn't. And even though Ellen could understand why it might be difficult for him to visit Fender's Field in person, she couldn't understand why he hadn't got a message to her. As Ellen sat by her father's bedside, she realised she missed Joe more and more.

On the other hand, Ellen tried not to think of Edward at

all. Because every time she did, she felt more and more confused and upset. There must have been a reason why his father had never come to the circus, but in that case why hadn't Edward returned to explain? Or even write a letter? Or had it really just been a dreadful delusion on her part? Ellen pushed away the thoughts like she had done so often before. It was all too painful, and she knew she couldn't help her father if her own mind was troubled.

By the end of the third week, Fred's burns were beginning to heal over properly. But as they healed, he became more and more agitated.

"It's no good, Norah," he muttered over and over again. "Spangle's is finished. We'll end our days in the workhouse!"

"Hush, Fred!" said Norah. "You're getting stronger all the time. Summer is coming. We'll be away on the road soon."

But Fred only shook his head and began to pick at his scabs.

"Stop it, Father," pleaded Ellen. "They'll go bad if you fuss with them."

The next day Fred woke up yelling and thrashing about on his pallet. His forehead was hot and dry and even though he was thirsty, he couldn't swallow anything.

Ellen peeled back a bandage. The burns were yellow and stinking. What she had feared most had happened.

All that day Norah and Ellen sat with Fred. They watched

without speaking as he grew steadily worse. By evening, he no longer recognised either of them.

"He's dying," whispered Norah. "Now it's too late to say good-bye."

She had grown thin and haggard. Her eyes were black with exhaustion. "Go to bed, Mother," said Ellen. "I'll keep watch." She took her mother's hand. "The fever might leave him. We mustn't give up."

That night Ellen wrapped her father in a cotton sheet soaked with lavender oil. His chest was too raw for a mustard poultice. She covered him in thick blankets and banked up the stove.

Sam crept in and handed her an orange and a piece of bread.

"Why does Pa look like a mummy?" he asked. He wiped away the sweat that was trickling into his eyes. "Why is it so hot in here?"

Ellen buried her head in her hands. "It worked for Claudius."

Fred stumbled through a desert of red and gold sequins. They burned his feet as if he was walking on embers. He tripped and fell. The sequins filled his mouth and scratched his eyes. He tried to push them away, but they cut into his flesh like a thousand glass splinters. He tossed and turned and howled in agony.

A shadow passed over the ground. Fred looked up and

saw an angel hovering over him. He crawled under the cool shadow of her wings. The shadow turned into a pool of soothing water. Slowly his pain went away.

Fred opened his eyes. He was in his old wagon. The shining copper pan hung on a hook by the stove. The red and white patchwork quilt covered the bed that all his children had been born in. Laughter rang out behind him. Fred turned. It was the sound he missed more than anything else in the world. Lucy stood in front of him.

Lucy walked towards him. She caught a tendril of her long red hair and wrapped it round his finger. She pulled him close to her. Fred felt the warmth of her body and smelled the scent of her skin. Lucy stood on tiptoes and cupped her father's face. "Live for me," she said.

Fred sat up. The room was hot and the air smelled of lavender. Lucy's presence was all around him. "Where are you? Where are you?" he cried.

Ellen put her hand on her father's forehead. It was damp and sweaty. The fever had left him. "It's Ellen," she said quietly. "You're going to be better now."

"But Lucy—" Fred looked into Ellen's eyes. They were huge and black in her long, pale face. Somewhere in his mind, he knew she had saved him. He clutched her hand. "God bless you, darling," he muttered. He turned on his side and for the first time since Lucy's death, he sobbed and sobbed, as if there was an ocean of tears locked up inside him.

# TWELVE

"SAGO PUDDING!" FRED SPLUTTERED AS HE HEAVED HIMSELF UP in bed. "That's nursing mothers' grub. What do you think I am?"

"A sick old showman," said Ellen. She picked up a pitcher of veal broth and refilled her father's empty mug. "And one who has to stay in bed."

"I won't be fussed over," said Fred. He spooned the sago pudding into his mouth and gulped down the broth. "I'll get up when I want."

Ellen straightened the red and white quilt that Sam had saved from the fire.

Fred was back in his old wagon. The circus hands had worked day and night to mend it. Now it had a new roof and door. The inside of the wagon was different too. The walls were painted white and there were daffodils on the table. The picture of Fred's mother hung in its usual place by his bed. Beside it was a picture of Lucy.

Fred hadn't said anything when he woke up that morning and saw it in front of him.

"I thought she might keep you company," said Ellen. She turned to cut up a hunk of bread for his breakfast.

Fred looked at the photograph. Lucy was posing in her new costume. She held out her sequined skirt, smiling like a child in a party dress. Neither of them had spoken of the night Fred's fever broke and his terrible sobbing that had lasted until dawn. Ellen knew they never would.

Fred held out his hands and Ellen passed him the photograph. He ran his finger around Lucy's face. "She looks just like her grandmother," he said proudly.

Sam knocked and walked into the wagon. He was dressed in the ochre yellow tights and silver waistcoat Ellen had made him for his new act with Jake. He sat down by his father's bed. It was an odd feeling for Sam. For the first time ever he looked forward to being with his father. They talked about Sam's new act and the penny shows he was putting on. Fred gave him tips and they were always useful.

"How's the juggling?" asked Fred.

"I can do five balls! Jake says if I keep at it, I'll get up to seven by the summer."

"Got a name for yourselves yet?"

"The Marvellous Mexicans." Sam hesitated. "What do you think, Pa?"

"Never had a Mexican in my circus before. But I ain't got nothing against 'em!"

Sam pulled a pack of cards from his pocket. "Fancy a game of whist?"

Fred heaved himself up on his bed. "That's more like it."

"I'm off to the market." Ellen put on a plain bonnet and

shawl. Sam turned, hearing the disappointment in her voice. It was the same every day he came. He knew she was hoping for a message from Joe, but Sam hadn't seen him, nor had he heard anything of him. He looked into his sister's pale face and shook his head imperceptibly.

She nodded and walked out the door.

Ellen walked into the street and breathed in the fresh air. It was the first time she had been out of Fender's Field for weeks. Somewhere a barrel organ played a marching tune. It made Ellen remember that she hadn't been on the back of a horse since the fire.

While Fred was ill, Norah decided to keep the circus going with half of their usual acts. Sam showed his Happy Families Cage and put on the Battle of Trafalgar when he had enough goldfish. Jake and a new partner called Charley Goff performed, but they were really practising new routines for the summer. And of course Ludwig boxed with Lord Rowley. If it hadn't been for the kangaroo's popularity, money would have been very tight indeed. When Fred had gone down with the fever, a rumour went round that the summer season would be abandoned.

Word came to Ellen from the Bunch of Grapes that the only one pleased with the news was Jeremiah Morgan, and she made very sure that Fred didn't hear a word of it. But now that the circus folk could see that he was getting stronger every day, there was a keen sense of expectancy in

Fender's Field. Everyone believed the circus would leave for the summer tour as usual.

Ellen turned up Eel Street and walked past a row of tumbledown houses towards the market. She felt the excitement too. For the first time ever, she was looking forward to getting away.

Edward de Lacy's heart soared in his chest when he saw Ellen with her shawl and basket turn into the street. For a week he had waited in an alleyway by the old theatre, hoping for a chance to talk to her on his own. He knew from overhearing snatches of conversation that Fred was recovering well and that Ellen had nursed him night and day. In his mind he felt her cool hand soothing his own hot brow as he bided his time in the shadows.

Now Edward followed Ellen as she walked quickly past a group of children throwing stones at a wall.

"Polish yer shoes, mister?" As soon as he passed the children, they stopped their game and surrounded him. "Them's good leather, them is." Edward knew better than to try and shake them off. He chucked a sixpence as far as he could throw it and hurried away from them.

Ellen was standing in front of a vegetable seller when he finally caught up with her. He ducked back into the shadows and watched as she smiled and filled her basket with carrots and turnips and apples. When she turned to go home, Edward darted into the street.

A boy was shouting, "Oranges! Ripe for eating! Sixpence a bag!"

Edward stopped. Fruit would be a good present to give Ellen for her father.

"A dozen of your finest, please!"

The fruit seller's boy took one look at the gent in the floppy bow tie and sold him the shrivelled ones he had boiled the night before to make them look plump.

Edward stuffed the oranges awkwardly into his pockets, then ran down the street.

"Ellen!"

She spun around. "Edward! What on Earth are you doing here?" She awkwardly smoothed her jacket and tried to brush some imaginary mud off her skirt.

"My darling! I feel so terrible," said Edward quickly. "But I didn't abandon you." His hands fluttered by his side. "My father was on the packet for Paris by the time I got home."

Ellen moved away so the stallholders couldn't hear them. Edward followed her, talking rapidly. "I felt so dreadfully guilty, I didn't know what to do!" He stepped in a pile of rotting cabbage leaves and felt them squelch under his soles. "I came back to explain but then I heard Jake talking about another doctor who was on his way and I—" He stared down at the cabbage leaves stuck to his boot. "I thought it best to respect your family's privacy."

By now they were in a wide street with neat, red brick

houses on either side. Children in clean pinafores were playing with a ball in the street. The air smelt faintly of roast
meat.

"Please tell me I did the right thing!" Edward stopped
and took Ellen's hand. "I've been in such agonies, Ellen. I
truly have!"

Ellen looked into Edward's blue eyes. He looked as if he
was almost in tears. She felt his fingers tighten around her
wrist.

"You might have written," she said.

Edward hung his head. "Will you ever forgive me?"

Ellen looked up. An east wind was blowing. The air was
filling up with wisps of yellow mist. Across the line of roofs
and chimneys, the sky was turning from white to dirty grey.
Ellen pulled her shawl around her shoulders.

"Fog's coming, Edward," she said. "We must both get
home."

"Say you'll forgive me! Please! I can't paint. I can't sleep!"
Suddenly he remembered the oranges. "Give these to your
father! They were the best the fruit seller had."

Ellen saw immediately that the oranges had been boiled.
In Drabble Market, there was only one lad who did that. An
odd feeling took hold of her. She had already asked Edward
what he was doing there and he hadn't replied.

"How did you know I was in the market?"

The wisps of dirty mist were getting thicker. Edward's
mind went blank. He was frightened of fog. He would never

get across London if he didn't leave immediately. An omnibus clopped around the corner.

"Tell me, Edward."

There was no time to think up a good reason. Edward blurted out the truth. "I followed you." He reached for her hand. "It was the only way I could talk to you alone."

Ellen pulled back her hand. It made her feel dirty to think of him watching her when she didn't know. Why on Earth would he do such a thing? "Never follow me again," she said in a hollow voice.

Edward's face fell. "Dearest, I didn't want to disturb you when you were looking after your father."

"How did you know I was looking after my father?"

The omnibus drew nearer. Edward looked anxiously towards it. Ellen turned away from him. She knew the answer. He must have listened in on a circus worker's conversation.

"You'd best be heading home."

"When will I see you?"

Ellen shook her head. She couldn't think. "I'll write."

The omnibus passed slowly by. "Dear love!" Edward waved his hand wildly and clambered onto it.

A young boy passed by trundling a hoop made out of the band of a cartwheel. It was one just like Sam used to have. Ellen waited until the omnibus was gone and walked up to the boy.

"That's a fine hoop."

The boy looked up and grinned. "It's me brother's, but I'm better than 'im."

"Will you give these to your mother?" Ellen reached into her basket and took out the oranges. "Tell her they've been boiled, mind."

The boy stared at the oranges. He'd only eaten one once, when his dad took him to the circus. "Thanks, miss. Thanks!" He looked up into Ellen's face. "Good luck, miss!"

As he ran down the street, a pack of children appeared out of nowhere and began to chase after him. "Gi' us one! Gi' us one!"

Swirls of fog floated in the air. They were darker yellow now. Soon they would thicken into a stinking, choking mist. Ellen slung her basket over her arm and walked quickly down the street.

Ellen wasn't the only person in the market that day. Joe Morgan had stopped to buy a new pair of boots from the shoemaker on his way to meet with friends and play dice in the tavern. He had noticed Edward as soon as he stepped out of the alley. Despite himself he followed him.

Over the past weeks, Joe had found himself thinking of Ellen constantly. When Sam had given him her message, he knew he should have replied or, even better, gone to see her at night when there was less chance of being recognised. But he couldn't bring himself to do either. And the next time he'd met Sam, he had seen immediately the embarrassment in the boy's face. Ellen had obviously been asking after him. But what was Sam to say when Joe had given him no message for her? After that he took care to avoid the lad.

Joe told himself the same thing as he had the night he had come to the wagon when it seemed Fred was going to die. Any comfort he might give Ellen could weaken the strength she needed to save her father. But Fred was getting better and Joe still couldn't bring himself to see Ellen. This time, he told himself that he didn't want to distract her just as her life was falling back into place.

Now Joe had watched as Edward de Lacy's hands fluttered nervously at his sides and Ellen stood frozen-faced and unmoving in front of him.

Then he watched as Edward scrambled onto the omnibus. As he stumbled down the aisle and swung himself into an empty seat, his face was bright and excited like a child on an outing.

The moment the omnibus turned the corner, Joe saw Ellen give away the oranges. He could tell from the slump of her shoulders that whatever had been said between them had upset her. Joe felt fury surge through him. He wanted to run to Ellen, but he didn't. He wanted to comfort her, but what good would he be full of an anger that was nearly choking him? He turned away and when he looked again, the mist had swallowed her up.

Suddenly Joe was gripped by despair. The thought of drinking and playing dice sickened him. He turned back and headed home.

# THIRTEEN

JEREMIAH MORGAN SAT AT HIS USUAL CORNER TABLE IN THE Unicorn Tavern and sank his teeth into a shank of roasted mutton. The meat was sweet and dark and delicious. As he stared out the window, he saw two men stuffing crusts of bread from the gutter into their mouths. They looked like scarecrows, with bony faces and ragged clothes.

"Dirty tramps," muttered Jeremiah. He wiped away the sticky juice that ran down his unshaven chin and reached for another boiled potato. Good news always gave Jeremiah Morgan an appetite, and the news that Fred Spangle was only just now up and about made Jeremiah as hungry as a horse. Now all he had to do was start up a rumour that Fred's sickness had returned. Everyone would assume he wouldn't be strong enough for the summer tour, and Jeremiah would be able to take his pick from the Spangle artistes. The feud between them would be over.

Because Morgan's Menagerie would have won.

Jeremiah licked his lips and eased another shank from the pot with his knife. While the meat cooled on his plate, he swallowed the beer in his mug. It wasn't just Fred Spangle's illness that was giving Jeremiah an appetite.

On the night of the fire at Fender's Field, Joe had been seen talking to Ellen Spangle. That on its own wouldn't have meant much, but then he'd found out that Joe had been to see Norah and Ellen after Fred's accident. And before that Joe and Ellen had been seen walking together in Greenwich. Jeremiah refilled his mug and smirked to himself. No one could accuse his boy of being slow off the mark.

Jeremiah Morgan bit into the juicy mutton. Since then he'd been paying close attention to his son. Sure enough, Joe was mooning about with a face like a dying duck in a thunderstorm. Once Jeremiah had followed him. Joe walked all the way to Tower Bridge and spent the morning staring down at the water.

It was an open-and-shut case as far as Jeremiah was concerned. His son was sweet on Ellen Spangle. Nothing in the world could be better.

Jeremiah slopped more beer into his mouth and made gleeful plans. It was a bad time for circus folk now. Winter savings were gone and everyone was pinning their hopes on the summer's takings. Fred didn't know it yet, but Jeremiah had already poached a tumbler called Charley Goff. Charley worked with Jake Naples. Of course, Jake was the better performer; but when Jeremiah had put the offer to him, Jake had cursed him for a thief and punched Charley in the nose for agreeing to take it. Jeremiah wiped his mouth. A time would come when Jake would regret he'd been so hasty. Still, tumblers were small fry. What Jeremiah needed was a class act.

Like Ellen Spangle.

At that moment, he saw Joe through the window. Jeremiah could tell he had something serious on his mind. The boy's shoulders were stooped and his face was stiff and pinched. He looked absolutely miserable. Jeremiah waved at a barmaid called Mog. "There's Joe!" he said. "Bring him in and get a plate and a mug of beer."

"Lucky I saw you, son," said Jeremiah when Joe sat down. "You looked starved." He pushed the pot of meat across the table. "Mutton's sweet as honey. Kent spuds, too. The floury ones." Jeremiah fancied himself an expert on potatoes. He lined up Joe's plate beside the dish. "You've always liked 'em."

Joe stared at the food. He hadn't eaten that day and he was hungry. He swallowed a mouthful of malty ale and bit into a mutton shank. He ate his fill while Jeremiah watched and said nothing. At last he sat back and pushed his plate away.

"Thought you was playing dice today," said Jeremiah. He signalled to Mog. Two more pots of beer arrived on the table.

Joe shrugged. "Changed my mind. Lost my lucky feeling."

Jeremiah fixed his son with his beady eyes. "Maybe you weren't looking in the right place."

Over the past few years, Joe had come to an understanding with himself about his father. He knew Jeremiah was a cheat and a villain, so Joe kept far away from the day-to-day business of Morgan's. Besides, he was more interested in training animals and sharpening the acrobatic skills he had inherited from his mother.

"Spangle's Circus," said Jeremiah suddenly. "Now that's a place I'm pondering on." He sat back on his chair and picked his teeth with the point of his knife. "We'll have the best of that tottering old fool yet!" He swallowed his beer and eyed his son. "And who knows what else?"

Joe looked at the greasy smirk on his father's face and wondered with a sick feeling what nasty gossip he was trying to tell him. Everyone knew about Fred Spangle. But they also knew he was over the worst and getting his strength back.

"Charley Goff's with us," said Jeremiah smugly. "So that's another new act for the summer."

Joe frowned. Charley Goff was a familiar name. Suddenly he remembered. He had accidentally met Sam a few days earlier and the boy had said that Charley no longer worked at Fender's Field. No one knew where he had gone, but he had a split lip and Jake had a face like a basin full of worms. Mind you, it had turned out well for young Sam. Jake had decided to train him up for the summer.

For a moment Joe wondered why Jake had kept quiet about Charley Goff if he knew his partner had deserted Fred Spangle for Jeremiah Morgan. Then he realised that Jake was trying to protect his boss. Fred would be apoplectic if he found out. More than likely, it would make him ill again. Disgust at his father's triumphant leer made the mutton shank turn sour in Joe's stomach.

Jeremiah leaned forward confidentially and put his hand on Joe's arm. "And a little bird tells me we might have a double act soon."

Joe put down his beer. "What are you talking about?" he asked in a cold voice.

"Don't come the hoity-toity with me," snapped Jeremiah. His face reddened. "I know what you and Ellen Spangle have been up to."

"And what's that?" Joe's voice was hard as stone.

Jeremiah stopped and thought quickly. The cosy man-to-man chat he had hoped for was not going right. He tried another tack. "Nothing to be ashamed of, son," he said. "You and Lucy. Well, that would have been dandy. But she's dead. It's only human to try for the sister."

Joe stared at his father. His mind was spinning. "How did you know about Lucy?"

Jeremiah chuckled. "I have spies everywhere. I know about everything."

Joe understood then that Jeremiah had known about Lucy from the beginning, and now the same spies were watching Ellen. He found he could barely speak. He said, "Are you suggesting there is some kind of understanding between me and Ellen Spangle?"

"O' course I am!" Jeremiah's crow eyes glittered. "She's soft on you. Charley Goff said so. You're just too beef-headed to see it!"

Joe pushed his chair backwards so it crashed on the floor.

Just hearing Ellen's name on his father's dirty beer-spittled lips made his whole body shake with anger. Joe picked up his beer and threw it in his father's face. It was all he could do to stop himself punching his teeth out. Then he ran through the crowded pub and pushed open the front door.

Outside, the mist that had been hanging in the air earlier had turned into thick fog. Joe couldn't see across the street. He stared wildly around him. He had to get away before his father came after him. It would end in a fight, and Joe was stronger than his father. He did not want to hurt him, but now anything could happen.

Patches of faint sunlight broke up the filmy greyness. A boy ran past with a torch. Joe grabbed him by the shoulder and pulled off his cap.

"Wot you do that for, mister?"

"Sixpence says you lead me to Morgan's on Porlock Green." He held the cap out of the boy's reach.

"Show us yer sixpence!"

"You get sixpence and your cap back when we get there!"

By the time they reached Porlock Green, the fog was thick, with a choking, sulphurous stink.

"You anything to do with the circus here?" asked the boy.

Joe shook his head. "Nothing." He paid the boy off and the light of his torch disappeared back into the murk.

Joe felt his way around paths that twisted in and out of the collection of shacks that made up Morgan's London premises. There was no crumbling theatre; only two houses

Jeremiah rented for the winter. He had a couple of acts. Crush-Bone Ivan the strong man and Cast-Iron Lil, who was a lady boxer. When she wasn't boxing, she dressed in turquoise velvet and played the barrel organ with a sailor called Whiskery Willy. Whiskery Willy had been a tumbler until he fell from the top of a human pyramid.

Cast-Iron Lil and Whiskery Willy had been together for as long as Joe could remember. They had brought him up after his mother died when he was six. Someone had to look after him. Jeremiah wasn't interested in his son until he was old enough to make decent money.

Joe turned the handle on the door of his own small wagon. He had refused the offer of a larger one from his father. He felt in the darkness for some matches and struck one against the rough iron stove. He took down a sooty paraffin lamp and lit it.

Joe hadn't collected much in his life. Now he wanted to leave most of it behind. He stuffed what few clothes he possessed into a hessian sack and tied it with rope so that he could sling it over his back.

He looked around the tiny, cramped room. There was a bunk, a chair, and a blanket box. In one corner there was a picture of his mother. She was standing on a high wire with a long balancing pole in her hand. One foot was pointed in front of the other like a ballet dancer. She wore black leather slippers that laced halfway up her calves. She looked completely composed, as if she was standing on a country bridge instead of a thick wire eighty feet up in the air. Joe pushed the picture to one side and slid his hands into a hole in the planked wall. His fingers gripped a soft leather pouch full of coins. In one part of his mind, Joe had always known he couldn't stay with his father, so over the years he had saved as much money as he could. He had almost eight guineas. It was enough to take him somewhere else where he could start again. He tugged out the pouch and pushed it down into the inside pocket of his waistcoat. Then he hefted the sack onto his shoulders and quietly shut the door behind him. Now there was only one thing left to do. He walked quickly down a narrow, muddy path to where the animals were kept.

Ten minutes later, Joe stood with his hand clenched around the greasy handles of his barrow. His Happy Families Cage was wrapped in canvas and wedged with what food he could find for the animals. Inside, they were quiet, except for the buzzard, who made a mewing noise as Joe trundled the barrow back down the path. His sack of clothes was slung over his back, along with half a dozen torches stolen from his father's supplies.

As Joe turned into the street, the sound of the barrel organ and pipes floated eerily through the fog. It was Cast-Iron Lil and Whiskery Willy. They always played together when there was nothing else to do. Joe's heart lurched in his chest. There was no time to say good-bye to them. Jeremiah would be back any minute.

ß  ß  ß

Two hours later Joe reached Fender's Field and pushed the barrow over the bumpy grass. He met Ludwig, who was setting out for an evening at the Bunch of Grapes. When the fog was this bad, the only places that did well were the pubs, even though the greyness seeped through every crack in the windows and the rooms looked as if they were filled with smoke.

Ludwig didn't ask Joe why he had come. He took charge of the Happy Families Cage and promised to tell Sam the next day. He shook Joe's hand, and the two of them set off in opposite directions into the choking, foggy night.

Joe's only plan was to put as much distance between himself and Jeremiah as he could. He decided to head towards Holborn. When the fog cleared, there would be omnibuses to take him to the railway station at King's Cross.

He made his way slowly through the tangle of narrow alleyways. While the fog had been useful in keeping Jeremiah off his trail, it was a dangerous time to be out in the streets. On nights like this, thieves thought nothing of cutting a few throats while they went about their business. Joe stopped to shift the sack on his back. Muffled footsteps behind him stopped too.

Joe's heart hammered in his chest. Even though he couldn't see his hand in front of him, he set off as quickly as he could. If he could get to Whitechapel Road, it would be busier and safer.

ઈ   ઈ   ઈ

Joe woke in a gutter. His head throbbed, and when he touched his cheek it was sticky with blood. He felt in his waistcoat pocket. His pouch was gone. The torches and his sack of belongings had been stolen too. The fog was so thick it was impossible to know where he was. Joe felt gingerly around him. There were open sewers in the gutter. If he took a wrong step, he could fall down one and get washed into the Thames.

He felt around in a circle. He was surrounded by muddy, greasy cobbles. Joe's heart went cold. He wasn't in the gutter. He was in the middle of a road. The sound of horses' hooves clip-clopped in the murk. That meant cabs were still about. He could be run over any minute. He got onto his hands and knees and crawled across the cobbles until he bumped into a wall. That moment a cab rattled past him.

Joe had to get off the streets. He didn't believe much in God, but as he pulled off his right boot and pushed his hand inside, he prayed harder than he had ever prayed before.

Underneath the leather sole, his shaking fingers found a crown taped down beside four sixpenny pieces. It was something Whiskery Willy had taught him. *Insurance, lad. Never forget it.* Now he could afford to spend a night in a doss-house.

As long as he could find one.

Joe stood up shakily and started to walk.

All around him, men and women moved like ghosts through the fog. Some were pushing barrows. Others led donkeys and carts. He saw the glow of a torch on a street corner. A beggar was slumped against a wall, his head hanging between his knees. Joe squatted beside him.

"A penny is yours if you take me to a lodging house."

The beggar looked up. In the sickly light from the torch, Joe could see the skin was stretched tight over his bones.

"I can't move, mate," he muttered. "Me legs ain't good."

He sat up and pointed down the street. "Nearest doss-house is up there, second on the right. Six doors down from the Velvet Pig." The beggar peered into Joe's face. "Stay away from the Pig. The tarts'll steal what you don't know you have." Joe put a penny in the beggar's hand.

The doss-house stank worse than any animal cage Joe had ever known. It was a long, low room lit from a couple of tallow torch brackets. Narrow tables stuck with candles lined the walls. Ragged men sat on rough benches, scooping a foul-looking mixture into their mouths. No one used the knives and forks that were chained to the tables. In the middle of the room, beggars of all ages snapped and snarled at each other like dogs. Some swapped old coats for tobacco, others cracked boots for gin. A young woman was being sick under a table. Joe felt bile rising in his own throat.

"Get on with ya," squawked a hag in a dirty apron. "There's more where you come from." She shoved Joe in the small of the back and sent him sprawling into a dark corner of the room.

It was a lucky shove. The corner was empty, or at least Joe thought so until a tall, thin man in a black suit uncurled from the wall. He stood up and held out his hand.

"Henry Rucket," he said simply. "Engraver turned ratter."

Joe looked at the man's face. It was long and thin and criss-crossed with lumpy scars.

"Joe Morgan."

Joe took the man's hand and shook it. Now that he had no money, he had no choices. "Is there money in the ratting business?"

"Only if I beat the dogs."

"You mean you fight the rats with your teeth?" Joe shuddered. He had heard stories of such fights but had never believed them. The thought that a man could thrust his face into a pile of squirming, biting rats, snapping and snatching like a terrier, revolted him.

Henry Rucket pulled back his lips to show long, narrow teeth. The raised scars on his face seemed to move when he smiled. "It's a hard way to make a living, but better than starving. What happened to you?"

"I was robbed in the street. They took everything I had."

They sat down together and slumped against the wall. Henry Rucket pulled out a flask of rum. "Drink?"

"Thank you."

Henry Rucket filled two tin cups half-full and gave one to Joe. "It isn't often I meet a young man with good manners." He drained his cup and refilled it. "Mind if I give you some advice?"

"I'd be grateful."

"Sleep with your boots against the wall. Else they'll have 'em off you and you won't feel a thing."

A desperate weariness washed over Joe. He had never had such a painful, miserable day in his life. He finished his own mug. "I'm sorry. I'm poor company tonight."

"Sleep, lad," said Henry Rucket. "I'll watch out for you."

Joe's head dropped on his chest and he fell sideways onto the filthy earthen floor. As he fell into a deep, black sleep, he felt Henry Rucket wrap a coat around his shoulders.

All night, he dreamed of Ellen.

# FOURTEEN

ELLEN WATCHED LUDWIG BRUSH THE LONG, PALE FUR DOWN the front of Lord Rowley's neck. The kangaroo stared back at her with wary eyes.

"You are making my kangaroo nervous, Ellen," said Ludwig calmly. He moved sideways and began to brush Lord Rowley's back. "What do you want?"

Ellen knew from Sam that Joe Morgan had arrived a week ago on that foggy day and had given Ludwig his Happy Families Cage. Sam hadn't heard from him since. No one had. For the first time, Ellen went from feeling sad and worried to feeling desperate. She had to talk to Joe. He was the only person she could trust.

Since her father's accident, Ellen had gone over and over in her mind everything that had happened between her and Edward. And each time, she felt more and more confused. Something wasn't right, but she didn't know what it was. Once Joe had told her that although he loved Lucy he had never felt he knew her. Now Ellen felt the same about Edward.

Ellen groaned inadvertently. Lord Rowley glared at her and flattened his ears.

"You're upsetting my kangaroo," said Ludwig. There was an edge to his voice and Ellen heard it. He knew why she was there, but he wasn't going to make things easy for her. If she wanted to know about Joe Morgan, she would have to come out and ask.

"Did Joe say where he was going when you saw him?" said Ellen at last.

Ludwig put down his brush. "Joe Morgan looked like a bird with no feathers to fly on," he said. "My guess is he fights with Jeremiah."

"Why?"

"Why?" repeated Ludwig. "How should I know? Ask the old vulture yourself."

"Me?" cried Ellen. "That's impossible! How could *I* go to Morgan's?" Tears welled up in her eyes. "If Father found out, he'd go mad."

Ludwig picked up a currycomb and began to loosen the dried mud that clung to Lord Rowley's haunches. "There's a yellow wig in my travelling box."

Jeremiah Morgan glared at the yellow-haired doxy standing in front of him. So this was the company Joe was keeping. Stupid little bugger. A class act like Ellen Spangle wouldn't look twice at him if she ever found out.

"I ain't my son's keeper," he snapped. "What do you want him for?"

The three teeth Ellen had blacked out tasted of charcoal

in her mouth. Her cheeks were rouged and she wore a huge cheap velvet bonnet and a grubby polka skirt that she had covered with mud.

She grinned a crimson smear of lipstick.

"Lush Babs wants 'im," she cackled. "Urgent business."

As she had hoped, Jeremiah presumed Joe owed money. "He ain't been here for a week," he snarled. "An' he ain't coming back."

Jeremiah swung round like an angry bull and stamped off across his yard.

"Wot you doing here, Ellen Spangle?" asked a deep voice.

A huge woman with a lard-coloured face was standing in front of her. From what Joe had told her, Ellen knew she was looking at Cast-Iron Lil.

"Don't worry. I ain't giving you away." Cast-Iron Lil grinned toothlessly. "Though how you fooled the old bastard looking like that, I'll never know." She rolled her eyes. "Good boots, no paint around the eyes." Cast-Iron Lil stroked Ellen's glossy black hair that showed under her wig. "And as for these frizzy yellow curls o' yours..."

Now that Ellen knew her disguise wasn't convincing, she was terrified. If she didn't look the part, she should get away fast. "I need to find Joe," she said quickly. "What's happened to him?"

"They had a falling-out in the boozer. Joe chucked his beer in the old guy's face. No one's seen him since." Cast-Iron Lil looked into Ellen's face. All the paint in the world couldn't hide her beauty. "He took his Happy Families Cage."

"I know. He left it with my brother."

Tears hung in the folds under Cast-Iron Lil's eyes. "Tell me if you hear anything. He was a son to me and Willy."

"Who can I trust?" asked Ellen quickly.

"Foley at the Grapes. And if we hears anything we'll let him know too." Cast-Iron Lil jerked her head sideways. "You'd bet-. ter be gone, lass. 'E's coming back and 'e don't look pretty."

Ellen turned to see Jeremiah loping over the muddy ground towards her.

She ran as fast as she could, blessing the tough soles of her own boots.


Norah didn't ask Ellen where she had been that afternoon. As Fred began to recover, she had watched Ellen become more and more distracted and unhappy.

"We've got to do right by the lass, Fred," said Norah one evening when they were alone. "She's done her best by us."

Fred stared down at the braided rug on the floor. During the time that Ellen had looked after him, he had grown to love her deeply. And even though Norah had told him about Ellen's hope of becoming a teacher, over the past few weeks he had prayed she had forgotten all about it. The idea of her going away was unbearable.

"She's trapped here, Fred," said Norah. "If she wants to go, we must let her. I left my father for you."

"But you didn't leave the circus," cried Fred. "The lass is a talent! I never knew how good she was until—" He looked down at the braided rug again. The colours blurred into one another.

"She has to be free to choose," said Norah. She put an extra chip of sugar into his tea and stirred it. "Tell me what I shall say to her."

Fred sipped the sweet tea. When he looked up again into his wife's face, his eyes told her what she needed to know.

A week later Ellen sat in her room, reading and rereading a letter from Edward. It was all about his journey home that foggy day. It had been such an adventure. He'd heard ghostly voices calling in the streets. Cabs loomed out of nowhere. Lines of torches passed by him in the mist. It reminded him of Venice during the Carnival. *One day, my dearest, we'll go together.*

The door wasn't closed, so Ellen didn't hear Norah come into the room.

"Ellen."

Ellen looked up. Norah saw confusion on her daughter's face, and the letter in her hand. The paper was thick and creamy, so she knew who it was from. Norah sat down on the bed beside Ellen.

"Your father and—," she began. Suddenly she couldn't go on. It was too hard. Unlike her love for Lucy, which had often been difficult to find, Norah had loved Ellen from the moment she was born. Like Fred, she couldn't imagine a life without her.

"What's wrong, Mother?" Ellen stood up, and Edward's letter dropped to the floor.

"Nothing."

"What are you trying to tell me?"

Norah took a deep breath. "That your life is your own." She hesitated as her eye caught the letter on the floor. "Whatever you decide to do, you have our blessing."

Ellen began to tremble uncontrollably. These were the words she had wanted to hear for so long. Yet now that she'd heard them, she felt as if she was falling forwards over a cliff.

Norah got up. "I took my chance when I saw it," she said, fighting to keep her voice steady. "You must take yours." She touched Ellen quickly on the shoulder. It was all she could do. Then she turned and left the room before Ellen could see her face.

Ellen sat perfectly still. She looked down at Edward's letter lying on the floor. The address was printed at the top. *30 Leominster Villas, Notting Hill.*

Ellen changed into the blue wool skirt and jacket Lucy had given her. She fixed her hair and pinned on the little black hat. Then, before she could change her mind, she quickly walked out of the door.

# FIFTEEN

THE OMNIBUS TRUNDLED SLOWLY UP REGENT STREET. ELLEN stared at the wooden pavements crowded with people. Men strode alone, elegant in pin-striped morning coats, canes swinging from their hands. Beautifully dressed women walked, arm in arm, stopping every now and then to look at the window displays. Behind them, maids in black uniforms struggled with armfuls of brown paper parcels. Ellen looked down at her blue jacket and striped skirt with increasing dismay. What had seemed presentable in the East End was drab and unfashionable here.

She changed omnibuses at Tyburnia, where a man was selling white poodles tied to a lamppost. There must have been twenty of them yapping and dancing on their back legs. Ellen watched as a young girl and an older woman stopped. The girl pointed at the smallest of the poodles. The woman, who looked like a governess, shook her head and dragged the girl away.

They rattled along Bayswater. Every time the omnibus stopped, Ellen fought back the urge to get out, cross the road, and go home. But she forced herself to stay where she was. She had to hold her nerve.

"Notting 'ill!" cried the driver at last. "Hold tight!"

Ellen stepped down into the muddy road and almost bumped into a man with a paunch and bushy side-whiskers. He was wearing a top hat. She stared at him. Perhaps this was Edward's father. The man returned Ellen's gaze with a disapproving snap of his eyes. Ellen went bright red. She knew exactly what he was thinking. Only the lower classes would be rude enough to stare. Once again she fought the urge to run away. Instead she went into the butcher's shop to ask for directions to Leominster Villas.

The lad looked at Ellen curiously. She wasn't a lady's maid but she wasn't a lady, either. Maybe she was a curate's daughter up from the country. They wore clothes like that, but mostly they weren't pretty. This one was. The lad gave her directions and watched as Ellen stood nervously at the edge of the street. Perhaps she had difficult tidings to tell her London relations.

Ellen crossed Notting Hill Gate and turned right towards Ledbury Road. Leominster Villas was on the left, the boy had said. She walked quickly, her eyes fixed firmly in front of her. She had no idea what she would do when she reached Edward's house. The thought of knocking on the door filled her with terror. All she knew was that there had been too many stories. She had to see something of Edward's life for herself.

The house was large, white, and square. A polished brass on the wall said SIR WINSTON DE LACY ESQ. PHYSICIAN. Through iron railings, Ellen saw a servant girl scrubbing a flight of wide stone steps. Two large sash windows, framed with swagged velvet curtains, gleamed on either side of the front door. The room on the right was some kind of drawing room. It was panelled, and a large cut-glass chandelier hung from the ceiling. The room on the other side was lighter and brighter. Ellen guessed this would be where Edward's mother held her visiting afternoons.

Suddenly Ellen remembered her father finding her sewing a new ribbon on an old bonnet. *A right afternoonified miss I've got for a daughter.* She pushed the memory away.

The front door opened and a pale, fine-boned woman stepped outside. She was dressed in a tailored lilac jacket. Her purple silk skirt was gathered up on one side and decorated with glossy braid. She looked like an exquisitely dressed Christmas tree fairy. Ellen stepped behind a clipped hedge so she couldn't be seen. A man's voice boomed from the darkness of the doorway. "Where's the carriage? Damn Riley! I won't be kept waiting!"

Ellen saw the servant girl curtsey and run. Then she realised that the man had seen her peering through the hedge. Ellen stared. He wore a top hat and a double-breasted frock coat. His face was square with blue eyes like Edward's, but it was cruel and overbearing. The man was undeniably Edward's father. But where Edward's face was weak, his father's was strong and arrogant.

To her horror, Ellen found she couldn't move as Sir Winston de Lacy walked towards her.

Their eyes met.

A nerve twitched on Sir Winston's forehead. Here was more than just a nosey servant. The girl's face was oddly familiar. It was her eyes. Suddenly Sir Winston remembered a sketch hanging out of a drawer in Edward's studio. He had pulled out the paper and looked at it. The face was badly drawn, but for once in Edward's useless career, the likeness was undeniable.

Ellen watched as Edward's father's face darkened. "What the devil?" he demanded.

The sound of his voice broke the spell that froze Ellen's body.

A crowded omnibus slowed down to let a brewer's dray cross the road. Ellen ran and clambered onto it.


"Ellen, me darlin'! Whoa! Hold up!"

Ellen started and looked around. It was as if she had been sleepwalking. She had no idea where she was. A donkey cart hung with dead chickens and rabbits passed within inches of her face. She stepped backwards and stumbled over a boy selling odd shoes on the street.

"Ellen!" cried the voice again. "Over 'ere!"

Ellen peered through the gathering dusk. On the other side of the road, Ada stood beside an iron oven, handing out baked potatoes. She shouted and waved again.

As Ellen ran across the street, she realised her feet were sore. She must have been walking for a long time.

Ada grinned and wiped her face in the steam from the pipe beside the oven. "What you doin' so far from 'ome, then?"

The grin disappeared when she saw Ellen's face.

"You look half dead, darlin'." Ada took Ellen's hand and put a potato into it. "Sink your snappers into that for a start."

Ellen looked down at the potato in her hand and her mind went back to another time, sitting with Ada's brother in the cold dawn. It seemed a long time ago.

"How's Adam?"

"Dead." Ada shook her head. "Always worried about his snakes catching cold. Then *he* gets one and snuffs it."

"Ada, I'm so sorry. You looked out for each other. He told me once."

"Not any more." Ada looked at Ellen sideways. "He asked after you."

"Me?"

"That linctus of yours," said Ada. "That's all he could swallow at the end."

Two men in neckties ambled down the street. They were just the kind to want something in their stomachs before drinking all evening. "Spud all over 'ot, gemmen!" shouted Ada. "Butter and salt all in!"

She sold two potatoes and turned back to Ellen. "Thing is, after Adam died, I got friendly with a shoe mender called George. Known 'im for ages, just never spoke to him. It started off 'cos he fitted Adam's clothes, so I swapped 'em for some boots. Anyway, George is a good sort and the end of it

is that we're off to Liverpool as soon as the roads dry out."
Ada's voice broke. "It's the snake, Ellen! I don't know what to
do with it. Adam got rid of the little ones. Couldn't swallow
'em no more. 'E got this python. I've kept it warm for his sake
and—truth is, Ellen, I've been asking after you everywhere.
You're the only person Adam said I could trust with it."

Ada looked into Ellen's face and her eyes were full of
tears. "I'd 'ate to think of it dying. I've 'ad enough of that
this winter." She sniffed and took a deep breath. "Will you
take it, Ellen?"

"Of course I will. And I'll give you something for it." Ellen
reached for her purse. "Big snakes cost money, Ada. You'll
need it for Liverpool."

"I don't want money," said Ada harshly. "You've been
good to me already."

"Then I'll swap it for some liniment when you come to
Fender's Field."

"I can't," replied Ada. She waved her arm around the busy
street. "This is the best pitch I've ever had. If I leave it, someone else'll nick it. Even for two hours."

Ellen watched as Ada's eyes slid across to an old leather
suitcase that was sitting beside the stove. "The snake's in
there, isn't it?"

Ada nodded. "It's alive an' everything. Last time I looked,
anyway."

Ellen picked up the suitcase. It was heavy, but now she
knew where she was, it was only a mile to walk home.

"Will you be all right?"

Ellen smiled. It felt like the first time in weeks. "Of course."

Ada dug about in her stove. She took out two big potatoes and put them into a tin box. "Take these in case you feel peckish later."

"But Ada! I don't have a basket."

"I ain't a barmy crumb," said Ada, rolling her eyes. She bent down and shoved the tin box into the suitcase. "Fact is, the snake could do with a warm-up."

Ellen burst out laughing.

The remains of a fire were smouldering in Ellen's room when she opened the door and crept inside.

"Where have you been?" demanded Sam. "You promised to take me to the Crystal Palace." He punched the candlewick cover on Ellen's bed. "I waited all day! Where were you?"

Ellen stared at Sam's furious face. What with Edward's letter and her decision to see where he lived, she had forgotten all about her promise to Sam. "Oh, Sam. I'm so sorry." She set down the case. "Maybe this will make up for it."

"Who wants an old suitcase?" asked Sam sulkily.

Ellen unpinned her hat and put it on top of the cupboard. "What if there were two baked potatoes and a python inside it?"

"Never!" Sam whispered.

"Would I lie to you?"

"Joe Morgan's turned rat catcher," said Sam suddenly. He

looked down at his feet. "I wasn't going to tell you 'cos you didn't show up."

Ellen felt her stomach turn upside down. "How do you know?"

"Nan Foley told me. Cast-Iron Lil told her."

"Where's Joe working?" asked Ellen, fighting to keep her voice steady.

Sam edged nearer to the suitcase. "Nan said he's been training terriers for some geezer he met in a doss-house. They get a guinea for every house they clear out. Nan said they're heading up north. There are more rats there, Nan said."

Sam stared at the suitcase sitting in front of the glowing fire. "When can I open it?"

Ellen pretended to straighten her bedspread to hide her face from Sam. Tears landed like fat raindrops on the thick blue cotton. She felt as if she had been punched in the stomach. No matter what happened, Ellen had always believed that Joe was enough of a friend to at least say good-bye. But perhaps with all the hurt and pain in her life, she needed him more than he needed her. In fact, maybe he didn't want to get mixed up with her at all. Yes, he had helped her with her father, but after that, she hadn't heard from him. Ellen roughly stuffed the corners of the bedspread under her thin mattress. She would be fooling herself if she thought there was any other reason for his coming to their wagon that night of the fire. Joe had been in love with Lucy. Not her.

"*Please* can I open it?"

Ellen surreptitiously wiped her eyes. But Sam didn't notice a thing. He was too busy staring at the suitcase.

"All right. But do it carefully." She lit a candle so they could see more clearly and bent down in front of the suitcase.

Sam undid the leather straps and took out the hot tin of baked potatoes.

"What's this for?"

"To keep it warm."

Sam groaned with delight.

Ellen saw the bright blue coat that Adam had worn the morning she met him folded up inside the suitcase. Sam picked up a frayed edge and began to pull it back.

A huge python lay in a pile of coils underneath. It was greyish green with a faint diamond pattern on its back. Its tail was ringed with black-and-white stripes. Ellen put her hand on the python's skin. It was smooth and cool. The snake didn't move.

"Do you think it's dead?" whispered Sam.

Ellen shook her head. "Hungry, maybe."

At that moment, the python lifted its head and shifted in the suitcase. A corner of an envelope appeared under its body.

"There's a letter," whispered Sam. He went to pick it up, but the snake moved again and he pulled back his hand. "I can't."

"Don't be afraid," said Ellen. "They don't bite." She ran her hand along the snake's body from behind its neck. When she got a good grip she heaved it over to one side and took out the envelope. Her name was on the front. She opened the envelope and took out a piece of lined paper. *Dear Ellen, Ada is writing for me. Please look after Luke. He eats mice. Thanking you extremely, Adam (Ada's brother).*

Sam stared at the snake. "Do you think I can teach him tricks?"

Ellen laughed. "You'll have to learn how to pick him up first." She folded back the bright blue overcoat and did up the straps of the suitcase.

"Can I leave him with you for the night?" asked Sam. "I've got a practice with Jake and it's warmer here."

Ellen handed Sam the tin of baked potatoes. "Of course you can." She picked up the candle and got to her feet. "He'll be company for me."

That night Ellen lay in bed but couldn't sleep. In the past when she'd tossed and turned, she called up the stories Edward had told her about his travels. Now when she thought of Edward, all she saw was his father in his frock coat and top hat with cruel blue eyes and an arrogant, overbearing face. What's more, she was almost positive he had recognised her, and the dark look on his face had been clear: He had not been pleased.

Ellen pulled the quilt over her head. She tried not to think of Joe. Knowing that he would soon be far away made her clench her fists with misery. She had never felt so alone in all her life.

# SIXTEEN

ELLEN WOKE UP TO THE SOUND OF HAMMERING AND MEN'S voices singing. Light poured around the edges of her faded pink curtains. She jumped out of bed and threw open the window. It was a warm and bright May day.

The suitcase was gone. Somehow Sam must have man-handled it out of the room without waking her. On the table was a pot of tea and a currant bun. That would be his present to her. Ellen opened her clothes chest and picked out a red pleated skirt she hadn't worn since the end of last summer. Beside it was a blouse that had belonged to Lucy. It had always been too big so Lucy had never worn it, but she had never let Ellen borrow it either. Now Ellen held the blouse in front of her. It was almost brand-new and made of heavy cream cotton. The collar and sleeves were edged with navy ribbon. She put it on and pinned her hair in a loose bun at the back of her neck. She drank her tea and walked outside with the currant bun in her hand.

Fender's Field looked like a carnival. Lines hung with glittering costumes were strung from wagon to wagon. All the horses were out and grazing on the new grass. Everyone was busy. Norah was bent over her sewing machine in front of her wagon. All around her, women shook out rugs and bedding and draped them over the hedges to air. Children ran back and forth with buckets of water.

In the far corner of the field, Fred was shouting orders as the big tent was pulled up to try it out for the summer. Now was the time to mend broken poles and tears in the canvas.

Fred waved at her, and Ellen realised with a shock that it was a greeting rather than a command. She waved back. Since he had recovered, Fred had changed. There was no sign of the vicious temper that had made his workers' lives so difficult. Now everyone said good morning when they saw him patrolling the field at dawn. Once or twice he had even been offered a cup of tea and a hunk of bread.

Ellen tried to ignore the sudden anxious fizzing in her stomach. She knew that so far she had tricked herself through the morning. She had spent time choosing what clothes to wear. She had sipped tea in the sunshine. The sugary taste of the currant bun was still in her mouth. Thinking about the change in her father made her think about herself. It was time to find somewhere quiet to sit down and work out what she was going to do with her life. She turned her back on Fender's Field and walked alone down the street towards the river.

It was only a slab of stone set back on the cobbled quay, but it served as a seat and looked out over the water. Ellen leaned back and crossed her ankles. A barge was unloading crates of tea. The air smelled of bergamot and cedar.

Ellen watched as a huge steamer made its way slowly up the river. LUXOR LINES was painted in bright blue letters on a wooden board at the prow. Men and women and children stood on the decks waving and cheering. It looked like they were coming home after a long trip away. Ellen closed her eyes and imagined the camels and pyramids and oceans of sand that these people had seen. She knew now she would never go to Egypt or Rome or Venice. It was a hopeless fantasy, just like her relationship with Edward.

Someone sat down beside her. Ellen turned and looked into Joe Morgan's face. She cried out and threw her arms around his neck.

Joe was as astonished as she was. He held her for a minute. Then Ellen pulled back, her face burning with embarrassment.

"Oh, Joe!" she cried. "I thought I'd never see you again! Why didn't you tell me where you were?"

Joe bowed his head. That morning he had woken feeling so sad and lonely that he thought he would never know the point of living again. He promised himself one last walk past Fender's Field in the hope that he would see Ellen before he left London forever. He waited until he saw her, then followed her down to the river. He couldn't help himself.

Now he could barely speak. He was afraid to hope that her relief at seeing him might be something more than concern for a friend. But he had to set things straight.

"I'm sorry, Ellen. I had to be on my own." Joe spread his

hands in his lap. "I had to think things through. I left word at the Grapes as soon as I could."

Ellen looked into Joe's face and saw a pain that she didn't understand.

"I know what I'm going to do now," said Joe.

A voice screamed in Ellen's mind. *Please don't go! Please don't leave me!* But she knew he must never know how she felt. He would despise her almost as much as she hated herself. How could she possibly have thought she was in love with Edward? How could she have been so stupid and stubborn for so long? She should have realised it was all wrong the day they visited Lucy's grave.

Ellen grabbed the edge of the stone slab and held it so tightly her fingers ached.

"Don't be angry with me," Joe was saying. When Ellen didn't speak, his worst fears were confirmed. "Please, please let me tell you what happened."

Ellen wanted to tell him she wasn't angry, but she couldn't trust her voice. Instead she sat without moving as Joe told her about the argument with his father. It was awkward for Joe, of course. He couldn't tell Ellen everything, in case she was still attached to Edward. Joe would rather have jumped into the river than have Ellen find out what his father had really said. So Joe skated over most of the quarrel and told her how he had gone back to Porlock Green to collect his animals. Then he described the night in the doss-house and his meeting with Henry Rucket.

"Next day, Henry bought a dozen terriers, and I trained them to catch rats," said Joe. "Of course, ratting comes naturally to terriers, but it's the teamwork that counts, and Henry soon got the hang of working them."

As Joe spoke, Ellen could hear pride in his voice. And she saw some of the sadness leave his face.

Joe thought of the last time he had seen Henry Rucket. It was two days ago, and his friend was wearing a new green woollen suit and a tweed cap. He held a cane in one hand and twelve leather leads in the other. Each was attached to a black-and-white terrier.

"You've made my fortune, son," said Henry Rucket.

"You saved my life, Henry," Joe replied.

They shook hands and parted.

"So what are you going to do now?" At last Ellen was able to speak.

Joe stared at the men scurrying about on the docks. Now that he was sitting with her, he knew he would do anything just to be near her for a little longer. He made up his mind to say what he had been thinking about for days.

"Would your father take me on for the summer?" asked Joe in a rush. "I'm a fair clown and a good rider." Joe looked into Ellen's dark eyes. "I'll never work with my father again."

Ellen thought she might faint. She buried her head in her hands so he couldn't see her face.

Joe's world shattered in that second. Everything was over for him. He was sure now that Ellen's affections were still with Edward. What he had dared to hope had been wrong and foolish. She didn't care for him. Not even as a friend. It had been a mistake to wait for her outside Fender's Field and follow her down to the river. Why should she care what he did? Suddenly it occurred to Joe that Ellen might have already decided to leave the circus before the summer tour. Now that Fred had recovered, her friendship with Edward might have become something more formal. The thought of Edward made Joe feel sick. He forced himself to speak. "I suppose Edward—"

Ellen looked up. Her face was blotchy and tears were pouring down her cheeks.

"I'm sorry," muttered Joe. "It's none of my business."

"No! No!" Ellen almost screamed.

Instinctively Joe put his hand on her arm. He was sure something terrible had happened, and all this time he'd been talking about himself. "Ellen—," he began.

"No, no," cried Ellen again. This time her voice was steadier. "You don't understand. I didn't understand until now." She grabbed his hands and held them. Tears spilled onto her lap. "Oh, Joe, I've been in such a muddle for such a long time. I love *you*. Not Edward." She sniffed and wiped her nose with the sleeve of Lucy's creamy blouse. As she thought of the blouse, she thought of Lucy. "But I tried not to tell you." Her voice broke. "Then I couldn't bear it any longer!"

Ellen looked into Joe's face. "Please tell me you don't hate me."

"Hate you?" whispered Joe. His world was whirling and twisting like a handful of ribbons in the wind. "Why would I hate you?"

"Because you loved Lucy," said Ellen in a stumbling voice. "Because—"

"Listen to me, Ellen." Joe unwrapped Ellen's fingers and put his hand on her cheek. "All the thinking I've been doing, I didn't tell you everything." He turned her face towards him. "I love you too. When Lucy was alive, I did think I loved her. But I was wrong." Joe shook his head sadly. "No one could ever love Lucy, she was too much in love with herself."

Ellen stared out at blurred boats on a blurred river. So many thoughts were crashing around her mind. Love fought with guilt. Joy fought with remorse. She knew that what Joe said was true. But she realised now that Lucy had understood her deluded relationship with Edward from the very beginning. *You're a circus girl. He's a gentleman. His fancy parents'd forbid it.*

Ellen rubbed her hands over her face again and again and again. With Joe beside her, she understood that Edward was a child. He always had been. Even so, the mistake had been hers from the beginning. She had allowed her vanity to override her common sense. She had been flattered by Edward's attention and an overblown sense of her own intelligence had brought terrible unhappiness to her family.

So it happened that even though the man she loved most in the world had just told her he loved her too, suddenly Ellen felt as if she was drowning in misery.

"Stop it," whispered Joe, reading her mind. He put his arm around her shoulders and pressed his lips to her hair. "The past is over now. We have to put it behind us."

"Wot you two lovebirds chirping about?"

A skinny boy covered in mud stood in front of them. He had a stick in one hand and three slimy canvas bags slung round his waist on a piece of filthy rope.

"Who's asking?" Joe smiled.

"I is," said the boy. "And a penny'll tell you why."

"What if I give you sixpence?"

"Oi'd be mighty obliged!" The boy dug into one of his bags and held out a bracelet with a charm swinging from it. "It'll bring you luck, mister." He looked at Ellen for the first time. "An' you, miss. I know it will."

Joe handed over a sixpence and took the bracelet from the boy's hand. The charm was a tiny prancing horse.

"What's your name?" asked Ellen.

"Luxor," said the boy proudly. "Named after a steamer, I am."

Fred slurped his cider noisily. "Seen our Ellen today, Norah?"

Norah shook her head. All day she had gone over and over the same thing. It was the moment she had taken a pot of tea and a bun to Ellen's room and seen the suitcase by the fire.

"That girl ought to be practising." Fred drained his mug and put it down on the table. "It's the new acts that draws the punters."

Norah turned away and pretended to fold a tea cloth. "Fred—," she began.

There was a knock on the wagon door. Norah crossed over to open it and stared down at Ellen and Joe Morgan standing hand in hand on the grass. The look on their faces told her everything. Pictures flashed through her mind like a magic lantern show. *Joe and Lucy. Joe with Ellen the night of the fire. Ellen's face when Joe disappeared. Ellen staring at Edward's letter.* Norah held out her arms. How could she have been so stupid?

At that moment, Sam clambered up the steps, dragging the suitcase Norah had seen in Ellen's room.

"Ma! Pa! Look what Ellen gave me!" He put the suitcase on the floor and began to undo the straps. "There's a python inside. He's called Luke! I'm going to train him! Ludwig says—"

Norah burst into hysterical laughter.

Fred Spangle looked at Ellen and Joe standing at the bottom of the steps and every hair on the back of his neck stood up. Fred knew as sure as eggs were eggs that quite apart from the look on their faces, which said only one thing, there was something else in the air. He knew from talk at the Grapes that Joe had left Morgan's and Jeremiah was calling him every name under the sun. Fred could hardly contain his glee. Joe was going to ask him for a job.

"Look, Pa! Look!"

Fred turned to see Sam struggling with a six-foot python.

"No, Sam! Not like that!" Ellen ran up the steps and took the python from Sam's hands. "Don't jerk him about! Hold his head firmly, otherwise he'll get nervous."

Norah watched, half-horrified and half-astonished, as Ellen draped the snake around her neck.

Fred hopped down the steps and took Joe by the arm. "I know what you're here for, lad, and I'd be happy to take you on."

"Joe's good with animals, Pa." Ellen jumped down beside them. "He knows how to ride, too." Her eyes shone like polished jet. It seemed she had forgotten she had a snake around her neck.

"Not like you," said Joe, smiling down at her.

"I could teach you."

"With a snake around your neck?"

"Why not?"

"Give me back my snake!" yelled Sam.

Fred held out his hand to Joe. "Welcome to the family, lad."

# SEVENTEEN

A WEEK LATER ALFRED MONTMORENCY SCRIBBLED A NOTE TO Edward and handed it to a messenger boy. Alfred had heard nothing of Edward since the night he had found him by chance in the streets. Of course, he'd meant to visit to make sure his friend had recovered, but there had been more pupils and the extra money helped his mother. Besides, Alfred knew Edward always suffered from an overactive imagination. He had just never seen him in such a state before. Alfred had even wondered whether he should write to Edward's father. In the end he had done nothing.

A hansom cab clattered under his window. Alfred watched as the two Miss Hendersons clambered out. They were his next pupils, but it was their custom to stroll down the street to take the air before their lesson. It also had the added benefit of cutting the lesson short by fifteen minutes, which was what they intended. For some reason Alfred suddenly thought of Pearl Rowley. He hoped the tattered edition of Keats's poems might encourage her to take up her lessons again in the autumn.

Downstairs a bell pull sounded. Giggling voices filled the

stairwell. Alfred took out a volume of Shakespeare's history plays. The Miss Hendersons had shown an interest in *Henry V*. They had heard the king was handsome and fearless. Alfred had agreed that was true. On that basis the Miss Hendersons had both promised to learn a speech from the play. Alfred's heart sank at the prospect of their recitations.

There was a rustling on the other side of his door. He stood up and opened it.

The fine weather persisted and Fred decided to put on a final performance before the summer tour. Since the fire, and during his illness, the circus had been working at half strength. This show would be a practice run for the next season. Huge new billboards had been painted and were nailed up on either side of the theatre doors. There were to be tightrope walking, acrobatic acts, clowns, and tumblers. But most exciting of all, The Amazing Sapphire Scarletta was performing with a brand-new act.

"That'll get them in," said Fred proudly to Norah one evening. His green eyes glittered. "What will old Morgan think? Now we've got 'is boy, eh?"

Norah looked up sharply. "Don't you start crowing, Fred Spangle. I won't have it." She picked up the small gold whip she always took with her into Claudius's cage and prodded him with it. They both knew that Jeremiah's fury was the talk of the Grapes, and there was even a rumour that Whiskery Willy and Cast-Iron Lil might join Spangle's Circus too.

"You'll turn our fortune against us with that kind of talk," said Norah in a fierce voice.

Another time, Fred would have bellowed at her. Now he picked up one of his black leather ringmaster's boots and began polishing it furiously. The truth was that he was worrying because Ellen refused to let him see what she was rehearsing with Joe. Only Ludwig was allowed in, and afterwards Fred had seen him shaking his head and muttering to himself.

Fred spat on his boot and rubbed harder. Since Lucy's death he no longer encouraged his performers to take risks. Now he was terrified that Ellen was going to do something dangerous to impress him.

"You'll rub a hole in that boot." Norah watched her husband chewing his lips. "Stop worrying, Fred. She's not Lucy." Norah picked up his other boot. "I'll do this one. You're making a right pig's ear out of it."

Alfred read Edward's note.

> *My dear friend,*
>
> *It has indeed been too long since we met and the fault is all mine. Would you join me for a light supper at the Sheaf of Barley on Saturday? Say six? I have an appointment later in the evening, but I hope this won't inconvenience you.*
>
> *With warmest regards,*
> *Edward*

The messenger boy looked around at all the books in the room and again at Alfred's threadbare grey suit. He couldn't understand. Why didn't the geezer flog the books and get himself a sharp jacket? "You clever, then?" he asked abruptly.

Alfred looked up from the note he had quickly scribbled to Edward, agreeing to meet at six. "Not particularly." He followed the boy's eye around the room. "I like books." He reached into his pocket. "Tuppence if it gets there tonight."

The boy nodded and ran.

Alfred got up to shut the door the boy had left open. After Edward's bizarre behaviour that night, he didn't have to be clever to know that after supper his so-called appointment on Saturday night could only be with Spangle's Circus. But why hadn't he said so? It was as if he had something to hide.

Alfred's mind was disturbed and he didn't know why. He decided to follow Edward when he left the pub after supper.


"Roll up, roll up! Ladies and gemmen!" Fred banged a gong and bellowed at the top of his voice. "This way to the Greatest Show on Earth! See the fearless Lion Lady! Likewise the renowned troupe of clowns and acrobats." Fred banged the gong again. "Thrill at The Extraordinary Amazing Sapphire Scarletta, performing this night and this night only." He jumped down the wooden steps in front of the theatre, banging the gong as he walked. "Walk up! Walk up! The show is about to commence!"

A huge crowd filled the street. Fred was amazed. He had never seen so many at this time of year.

"Who's the girl wot rides the 'orse?" asked a young man in a flat cap and necktie. "She's a wonder!"

"Sapphire Scarletta!" said Fred.

"That's the one!" said a lady. "I come to see 'er!"

"Everyone should have one, you know," said Edward as he chewed the last of his lamb cutlet.

"Have what?"

"A dead aunt," replied Edward, feeling thrillingly eccentric. "Independence. Freedom. That's the ticket, Alfred." He drained his mug of porter and put a sovereign on the table. "No, no. I insist. My treat. How's the novel going, by the way? Mama is always asking after it."

Alfred stared down at the sticky table. "Difficult business," he replied. "You make up a world, then you find out it doesn't work."

Edward leaned forward. "But surely if it's a made-up world, it doesn't matter if it doesn't work." He waved his hands in the air. "It's all an illusion, like a magician's trick."

Alfred shook his head. "Even made-up worlds must have a reason to hold together. Otherwise"—Alfred thought ruefully of his novel—"they fly apart like dandelion fluff."

"I don't know if I understand what you are saying," said Edward. "Real worlds and made-up worlds are all the same to me."

Alfred forced himself to smile. "I wouldn't want you as my doctor."

"Then perhaps I shall be in your novel instead," Edward said. He stood up and shook Alfred's hand. "You will excuse me, won't you? I did mention—"

"Another appointment?"

"Exactly." Edward's eyes gleamed as if he was a naughty child. "Another time?"

"Most certainly."

Alfred waited as Edward turned into a blind alley. Two minutes later he came out wearing a long black cloak with a high collar. Alfred shivered. Just as he'd thought. Edward was up to something.

The sound of the circus gong rang through the streets. Edward turned quickly down the road, and Alfred followed him.

Alfred paid his sixpence at the booth in front of the theatre and let himself be carried forward by the crowd into the hot, glittering theatre. He was in a state of utter shock.

Outside the portico, a suitable distance behind Edward, he had looked up at the enormous wooden billboards in front of the theatre. They were covered in garish paintings of snakes and lions and kangaroos. There was a man in a purple leotard walking a tightrope. A troupe of little dogs stood on their back legs and danced around a clown. Alfred's eye strayed over to the billboard on the other side of the door. A girl dressed in a fitted blue jacket and a skirt of silver net stood on the back of a horse. One hand held a pair of white reins. Her other arm was curved in the air like a ballet dancer. Her glossy black hair was piled high and held in place with a glittering comb. The painting was gaudy, but there was no mistaking the features.

Alfred was looking at Pearl Rowley.

He stood rooted to the spot. Someone shoved him forwards.

"Stop gawping! You'll see her soon enough!"

He stumbled forward. When he looked around again, Edward had gone.

Alfred sat wedged between a fat lady in a polka-dot dress and a small boy chewing an orange.

Alfred was dumbstruck. So these were Pearl Rowley's "unusual circumstances." He stared around the theatre to stop his mind spinning. In front of him was a large ring of sawdust. Beyond it a stage was hidden behind faded velvet curtains. A string of lights was draped around the tiered gallery of the theatre. An enormous gas-lit chandelier hung from the ceiling. To one side, a group of fiddlers and horn players idly tuned their instruments. Occasionally the trombonist blew a deep spluttering note, and all the children in the audience whooped with laughter.

The theatre was packed. Alfred watched as two clowns dragged young boys clear of the ring. "Now you stays *put*!" he heard one of them say. "Else your 'ead gets squashed by an 'orse's 'oof."

"Poor mites," said the fat lady beside him. "Their thruppence is as good as anyone else's." She wiped a film of greasy sweat from her forehead, leaving a dirty mark on her white handkerchief. "Mind you, them clowns is quite right. Anything can happen at the circus."

She squirmed on the seat and pushed Alfred against the young boy with the orange. He immediately elbowed Alfred sharply in the ribs.

"Wot a turnout, eh?" said the fat lady as Alfred bumped into her again. "And they had such tragics this winter."

"What do you mean?"

"Ain't you 'eard?" The woman peered at Alfred's inkstained fingers and good wool jacket. A clerk. No two ways about it. "No, p'haps you ain't," she muttered.

"I'd be obliged if you told me."

The woman smiled happily. "I likes a young man with manners. Now, where was I? Yus. First Seraphina Scarletta falls from her horse and breaks her neck. Then, if that ain't enough, the bleeding stables and wagons catch fire in the field over the way. O' course Mister Spangle should have died from his burns, him rescuing his 'osses an' all, but Miss Sapphire—that is, the late Seraphina's sister and being in real life—" At this point the woman dropped her voice as if she was telling Alfred something that was a secret known only to a few. "His daughter."

"Sapphire Scarletta is Miss Spangle?"

The woman narrowed her eyes. "That's wot I said."

"Then who is Pearl Rowley?"

"'Ow should I know?" asked the woman crossly.

Alfred decided to try one more time. "Do you know this circus well, madam?"

"'Corse I do. That's what I forgot to tell you on account of you askin' questions all of a sudden."

"I'm sorry."

"Don't matter. So after the fire and Mister Spangle's illness, the circus don't do much on account of Miss Sapphire, Ellen that is, looking after her pa."

"So tonight is a special occasion?"

"'Corse it is, you daft ink bottle!" cried the woman. "This is the last show before they leaves for the summer. And—!" She squirmed in her seat again. This time Alfred let himself get squashed rather than risk another jab in the ribs.

"What?"

"Miss Sapphire Scarletta has a brand-new act!"

At that moment, a handbell rang out and the orchestra began to play. As the great chandelier came slowly down, a hissing white light lit up the audience. Alfred looked across the rows of faces. Suddenly he saw Edward, sitting as near as possible to the ring. His cloak had fallen from his shoulders and he sat completely still, staring forward as if he was in a trance.

There was something so strange about the way Edward

looked that Alfred couldn't take his eyes off him. In the background he heard the ringmaster going through his patter. A clown came on, juggling five silver balls. Around him a troupe of excited little dogs jumped through hoops and leapt over barrels. Alfred turned away from Edward and watched the ring. As the clown bowed, a boy came up behind him. He was wearing a black and yellow baggy suit with a wide red ruff around his neck. He held out a stick, and the big clown pretended to fall backwards.

The crowd roared with laughter as the big clown turned to hit the little one over the head with his stick. As he raised his arm, the small clown suddenly whipped off the wide red ruff. The laughter died and turned to gasps of astonishment. A huge, glittering snake was wrapped around the small clown's neck. The big clown flipped over backwards as if he was terrified, while the boy paraded triumphantly around the ring with the enormous snake held high above him.

"Ladies and gemmen!" cried Fred. "The Marvellous Mexicans!"

Jake and Sam bowed and the crowd clapped and roared. Alfred watched as the ringmaster went up to the little clown and gave him an extra round of applause. Alfred felt his hands gripping the bench. He had never seen a live snake in his life, and he was horrified. How could the little clown be sure that the snake wouldn't strangle him?

Ludwig had given Sam the answer to that question. Luke was so full of mice, he was half-asleep.

As the clowns ran off, the ringmaster cracked his whip. It was time for the next act.

"And now, all the way from the Antipodes! Prince Ludwig of Bavaria and the one and only amazing Lord Rowley!"

Alfred was so surprised he jerked forwards in his seat. So here was Ellen Spangle's choice of surname. His gaze slid across to Edward. His friend hadn't moved.

Now the crowd was on its feet, yelling, as a dark, wiry man with a waxed moustache and a green waistcoat, aimed punches at a large kangaroo with leather gloves taped to his forelegs. "Hurrah! Lord Rowley! Give him one in the nose!"

It was as if the kangaroo understood every word. Alfred watched as the animal hopped about and made stab after stab at the wiry man's head. But each time, the man ducked and Lord Rowley bounced on his tail and tried again. Someone hit a gong. At the same moment, the dark man pulled out a handful of grass. As the kangaroo took it in his mouth, a lead was snapped to his collar. The crowd cheered. "Hurrah! Lord Rowley! Get 'im next time!" The wiry man flashed his white teeth in a big smile, bowed, and led the kangaroo away.

Two clowns ran in to tidy up the ring. A sharp sense of expectation filled the theatre. This was the moment everyone had been waiting for.

"Ladies and gemmen," bellowed Fred Spangle. He whacked his whip against his boots. "Please welcome the truly amazing Sapphire Scarletta on her incredible horse, Pearl."

The next moment, the young woman Alfred had known as Pearl Rowley galloped into the ring.

Suddenly a conversation he'd had with Edward all those months ago flashed through his mind. They had been sitting in the Sheaf of Barley and Edward had been asking him about his so-called mysterious pupil. At the time, Alfred remembered feeling vaguely uncomfortable. Then the rum had gone to his head and he'd told Edward her name. He had thought no harm could possibly come of it. Edward's enthusiasms were famously short-lived. Yet the more Alfred recalled the conversation, the more uncomfortable he became. He heard again the obsessive curiosity in Edward's voice.

Alfred felt physically sick. He guessed now that somehow Edward had struck up a relationship with Ellen Spangle. But how had he known where she lived? He would only know the name of Pearl Rowley. Then Alfred remembered the sight of a man bending down to tie his shoelaces at the end of his street. At the time, he had felt something odd, as if the man wanted to hide his face from him. Now he knew that man had been Edward. He must have been hanging about, hoping to catch sight of Pearl Rowley so he could follow her. There was no other explanation.

Alfred's brain felt loose in his head. What had the fat woman said? Ellen Spangle had nursed her father. He groaned out loud. For the first time he understood what had happened the night he found Edward on the streets. Edward had promised Ellen Spangle that his father would come. She would have been desperate and grateful to him. Alfred clutched his head in his hands. He himself had been the one who had persuaded Edward to abandon his promise. Even though Alfred knew Sir Winston would never have come, he might have acted differently if he had known the truth. Alfred looked over at Edward. He was leaning forward with an intense expression on his childish face.

Alfred jumped out of his seat and pushed his way through the crowd. He grabbed Edward's shoulders and yanked him round. "You bastard!" he croaked. "You deceitful, stinking worm! What have you done? What have you done to the girl?"

Edward blinked at Alfred. At first he had no idea who he was talking to. In all the times he had come to the circus, he had always kept himself to himself and no one had ever bothered him. Then he saw past the red angry face and recognised Alfred.

"Tell me the truth, Edward. Or I swear I'll break your stupid neck!"

"If you don't shaddup, I'll throttle the pair of yous!" yelled a woman behind them.

Edward stared. Why was Alfred so angry? Surely Alfred didn't think he would harm his beautiful Ellen.

Alfred tightened his grip on Edward's shoulders.

"You're hurting me, Alfred. Why are you behaving like this?"

"What is your understanding with Ellen Spangle?" asked Alfred in a low, furious voice.

Edward looked puzzled. Surely it was clear what he felt.

Then he remembered that he had decided not to tell Alfred his secret. Well, now he would know and that would be that.

"I adore her," said Edward in a faraway voice.

Alfred's hands slipped from Edward's shoulders. The man was a lunatic. He stumbled back through the crowd.

Ellen felt the roar of the crowd punch through her chest. She circled the ring, her feet planted on Pearl's heaving haunches. It was as if they were joined together through her thin leather soles. She flew over streaming ribbons. She sailed through fiery hoops. As she galloped, she twirled round on Pearl's back. First one way. Then the other. Then twice in a row.

The crowd gasped. Ellen threw back her arms and accepted their applause. As she passed the musicians, she clapped her hands. A new tune filled the theatre. Fred Spangle watched with his heart in his mouth.

It was the moment Ellen and Joe had rehearsed all week. The more they had practised, the more they realised how well they worked together and how much they loved each other. It was as if they had always known, they just hadn't been able to see it.

On the afternoon of the final performance, Joe and Ellen had walked down to the river. Neither of them spoke, but the silence was not uncomfortable. Ellen was thinking of Ludwig. The day before, he had taken her aside. What he saw of their rehearsals confirmed what he already knew: Ellen's ability to ride was positively uncanny.

"God has given you a great skill, Ellen," said Ludwig. "You have a duty to pass it on to your children. It is not like books you can teach to strangers."

"Why are you telling me this?" Then Ellen saw from his face that Ludwig knew about her lessons from Alfred Montmorency.

"Yes, yes," said Ludwig impatiently. "Lucy told me a long time ago." He shrugged. "Everyone is wrong-headed sometimes. But I think you have learned that now."

Ellen opened her mouth to ask him what he meant but shut it again. She knew he was talking about Joe.

And she knew he was right.

Now, as they walked to the river, Joe slipped his arm around Ellen's waist. "I want to talk to your father tonight, but I want to talk to you first."

Ellen caught his hand and laughed. "Gracious, Joe! That sounds serious!" She looked up at his face and touched his forehead. "You look serious too." Suddenly she stopped laughing. Something was wrong.

She led him to a slab of stone and they sat down. "Tell me, Joe. What is it?"

Joe cupped Ellen's face in his hands. She was so beautiful. Sometimes it almost hurt him to look at her.

"Will you marry me, Ellen? Before we go away? Before the summer tour?"

Ellen watched people passing in front of her. A young man with a flat cap leading a hound on a lead. A shabby old man clutching a shiny cane. A woman holding two small boys by the hand. Ludwig's words echoed in her mind.

"Will we have children?" she blurted.

Joe was so astonished, he burst out laughing. "I'll see what I can do."

Ellen went bright red and threw her arms around his shoulders.

They were still for a moment. Then Joe lifted up her face and kissed her on the lips.

"So, what do you say?"

Ellen looked into the face she loved more dearly than any other in the world. "Yes," she said.


The crowd roared as Ellen slid down Pearl's back and slowed to a canter. Something was going to happen. Everyone knew it.

Suddenly a tramp rushed into the ring and jumped onto the horse's back. The audience howled with dismay, but Ellen didn't move. Fred ran forward to drag the troublemaker out of the way. But he was too late; Pearl had taken off around the ring. Halfway around, Ellen and the tramp slowly rose to their feet. The crowd let out a great cheer. If this was a tramp, he was a damned good rider.

Fred Spangle let out a whoop of delight. "It's Joe bloody Morgan!"

At each turn, Joe pulled off a different layer of clothes. He changed from a tramp to a sailor to a masked bandit, and finally to a king with a cloak and a crown. They galloped a circuit while Joe shook out the cloak and waved the crown in the air. As if by magic, another crown and another cloak appeared.

Ellen became queen to Joe's king.

The audience went wild, They stamped their feet. They howled and screamed until their throats were hoarse. Then they howled and screamed again.

Fred was dumbfounded. He had never seen anything like it in his life.

Ellen pulled Pearl up and brought her into the centre of the ring. As she turned, she saw Edward. His face was blank and he was staring straight at her as if in a trance. She knew for certain then that he had never been in love with her. Edward had always been in love with Sapphire Scarletta.

Alfred watched Pearl Rowley's face as she stared at Edward. It seemed clear to him that her affections lay with her riding partner. A huge feeling of relief washed over Alfred. Even if he never saw her again, he knew that his silly indiscretion had not hurt her.

Somehow Alfred found himself wedged again between the fat lady and the boy with the sharp elbows. For the first time in his life, he stamped and roared with the crowd. He shouted and yelled until his voice was barely a croak. And, to his amazement, he felt tears on his cheeks. The fat lady turned and beamed at him. Perhaps the daft ink bottle had feelings after all.

Ellen raised her hand and bowed again and again. Beside her, Joe put his arm around her waist and pulled her towards him. Ellen turned and smiled at him. As she held her arm in the air, she felt the charm bracelet slide over her skin. She looked sideways and Joe followed her glance. The tiny prancing horse caught the gaslight and sparkled like a diamond above them.

"I love you," cried Joe.

Joy surged though Ellen like a shooting star. She leaned back into Joe's arms and let the circus carry her away.

§   §   §